SKUNNY WUNDY

The Iroquois and Their Neighbors
Laurence M. Hauptman, Series Editor

SKUNNY WUNDY
Seneca Indian Tales

Arthur C. Parker

Illustrated by George Armstrong
With a Foreword by Joseph Bruchac
With an Introduction by George R. Hamell

Syracuse University Press

Syracuse University Press Edition 1994
05   06   07   08   09   10   8   7   6   5   4   3

This book was originally published by George H. Doran Company, 1926.

The paper used in this publication meets the minimum requirements of
American National Standard for Information Sciences—Permanence of Paper
for Printed Library Materials, ANSI Z39.48-1984. ∞™

Library of Congress Cataloging-in-Publication Data
Parker, Arthur Caswell, 1881–1955.
[Skunny Wundy and other Indian tales]
Skunny Wundy : Seneca Indian tales / Arthur C. Parker ;
illustrated by George Armstrong ; with a foreword by Joseph Bruchac ;
with an introduction by George R. Hamell.—
Syracuse University Press ed.
p.   cm. — (The Iroquois and their neighbors)
Originally published: Skunny Wundy and other Indian tales.
New York : George H. Doran, [c1926].
ISBN 0-8156-0292-8 (alk. paper)
1. Seneca Indians—Folklore. I. Title. II. Series.
E99.S3P3 1994
398.2'089'975—dc20   94-27216

Manufactured in the United States of America

Contents

The One Who Listened

Joseph Bruchac

IT WOULD BE HARD TO IMAGINE A PERSON BETTER qualified to pass on the traditional stories of his Native ancestors than Arthur Parker. He proudly traced his descent not only back to Je-gon-sa-seh, The Mother of Nations, the wise woman who was one of the founders of the Great Iroquois League of Peace, but also to Handsome Lake and Red Jacket—two of the greatest of the Iroquois leaders of the early nineteenth century. It was the prophet Handsome Lake whose "Good Message" from the Creator revived the culture of the Seneca people after their decline following the American Revolution. It was Red Jacket who was regarded by many European Americans as the greatest orator —in any language—of his day. Arthur Parker's uncle was Ely Parker, a general in the Civil War and personal secretary to Ulysses S. Grant. Although their home may have been a humble one, there was true greatness and a world filled with the power of stories all around him.

Parker's home was always a place where stories were being told. He grew up in the late 1800s in the heart of the lands of the Seneca, on the Cattaraugus Indian Reservation in western New York. It was a common experience in his childhood for old men and old women to come and stay for long periods in their house and share legends around the fire at night. Welcomed as "grandparents," as "aunts" and "uncles," those elders had a special relationship with the children of the household, offering them guidance through their stories. And of all those who listened to those stories, no one listened better than the boy Arthur Parker.

Unless you have lived in an Indian community, as Parker did in those formative years, it may be hard for you to imagine the important place that stories held and still hold in Iroquois lives. Instead of telling other people what to do, a story may be told to help them see the right path to follow—or to recognize their errors. Instead of striking or shouting at a misbehaving child, a lesson story—perhaps even a story of how certain monsters come to carry away children who do not act properly—would be told. Even today, the old people continue the oral tradition, though they may now pass on the stories more frequently in English than in Seneca and they may also pause in their narration to watch where the wheel of fortune stops spinning—for television is also a part of contemporary Native American lives. The stories remain and are strong—vital threads that sew together the cloth of their culture.

Those stories, like the ones Arthur Parker listened to so intently that he would never forget them and would devote much of his life to passing them on to others, are often tales of pure wonder. When you hear them or read them, it is as if the rest of the world around you had ceased to exist. The old storytellers of the oral tradition and Parker, a storyteller who would use a pen with as much oratorical skill as old Red Jacket had used his voice when he would hold audiences spellbound, understood well that, in order to teach a lesson, it first had to be heard. Good stories have the power of drawing a listener in and teaching their lessons so effectively, so unobtrusively, that they insinuate themselves into the hearer's heart.

I firmly believe that, were it not for Arthur Parker's work in writing down and encouraging the telling of the old stories, much of the vital heritage of the Seneca people might not have survived that difficult period of the first half of this century, when most native people were keeping a low profile to survive or were even turning away from their traditional cultures —with the active encouragement of church and state. In all of his writing, from his biographies of Red Jacket and Ely Parker to his translations of Handsome Lake's Good Message and his compilation of numerous collections of traditional stories, Parker celebrated and drew attention to the traditional wisdom, oratory, and literary genius of his people. In an age when Indians were often either forgotten or labeled as merely exotic curiosities and "vanishing redmen," Arthur Parker was one Native American who was as eloquent, accurate, and prolific as any European American writer of his generation. He understood, far ahead of his time, what that timeless wisdom had to offer to his people and to the world. As a storyteller myself, I have learned and continued to learn from his example and from his writings.

The Seneca stories of animals (whose weaknesses and strengths are suspiciously like those of human beings) seem to have held a special place for Parker, perhaps because those stories are the ones that most children seem to love first and best. Everyone has known a boaster like Bear or Turtle or delighted in the way an animal story can explain how some things came to be. Instead of being pseudoscience, such stories are carefully constructed vehicles for teaching, made in such a way that memorizing them is almost as simple as breathing. And so it was with special delight that I learned of the reissuing of one of my favorite of Parker's books, *Skunny Wundy*. In it, Parker's voice is like that of one of those "uncles" who would come to stay and tell stories, the voice of an elder recognizing himself in the child who listens. One of my personal regrets is that I did not encounter this book, which had been out of print for decades, until I was in my late twenties. I wish I could have read it when I was a child.

But the next best thing to that is being able to recommend it to the children of another generation— native and nonnative children alike. Like the story- teller holding out his bag and asking a child to reach in and pull out the next tale to be told, it is my privi- lege to offer this book to you and to urge you to do as Arthur Parker did so well over a century ago, to listen. Listen well.

Gawaso Wanneh

ARTHUR CASWELL PARKER was a well-known anthropologist and museum director. He was born in 1881 and grew up on the Catteraugus Indian Reservation in western New York state. His father's family belonged to the Seneca tribe, and his grandfather was a leading sachem, or chief.

Before he was twenty, Arthur Parker had chosen anthropology as a career. After experience at the American Museum of Natural History and the Peabody Museum at Harvard, he went to the New York State Museum at Albany and was there from 1904 to 1925. For the next twenty years, Dr. Parker was the director of the Rochester Museum of Arts and Sciences. He retired in 1945 and died on New Year's Day, 1955, at his home atop a hill overlooking Lake Canandaigua in western New York.

Arthur Parker, whose Indian name was Gawaso Wanneh, wrote with authority on the Iroquois Indians. Three of his famous studies have recently been reprinted by Syracuse University Press.

The League of the Iroquois was a confederation of five tribes, sometimes called the Five Nations: the Mohawks, Oneidas, Onondagas, Cayugas, and Senecas, who lived across the width of what is now New York state. Historically, these Indians lived in long houses built of elm bark and their name for themselves literally translated means People of the Long House, Hodenosaunee (Ho-de-no' shaw-nee).

The Iroquois lands were in a region of forests and lakes. Hunting provided for many needs, and the Senecas lived on close terms with animals of the forest. Clan names, rituals, symbols, and stories reflect the importance of these animals to the Indians. Different creatures took on special traits, as the tales retold by Arthur Parker show. Fox and Raccoon are clever, while Rabbit is often easily duped. Bear is brave but not very bright, and Wolf is frequently a villain.

Turtle had a special place in Seneca mythology. The world was thought to rest on the back of a great turtle. Out of this turtle's back grew the Tree of Life with Sun at its top. George Armstrong, who knew Dr. Parker personally, chose the legend of the turtle for the cover design for this collection of Dr. Parker's stories for children.

Introduction

George R. Hamell

I CAN THINK OF NO BETTER INTRODUCTION TO IROQUOIS
[Seneca] oral traditions or "stories" than Arthur C.
Parker's *Skunny Wundy*, originally published in 1926.
Nor is there any better description of Iroquois storytelling than Parker's recollections of his boyhood on
the Cattaraugus Seneca Reservation in western New
York State and which is also reprinted here from the
book's original edition. Although addressed to a young
audience, *Skunny Wundy* is a collection of animal tales
that will delight young and old alike.

Oral traditions—whether myths, legends, or folktales—are more than just "stories." They are the way
by which a society communicates to its members the
order and meaning to be found in the world around
them. Through their example, "stories" serve as mod-
els to their listeners of what is and what is not proper
to think, to say, and to do within this world. Like
written histories, oral traditions often explain the pres-

ent in terms of the past, telling how "what is" came to be.

Although the message is always serious, the story by which it is conveyed may be humorous. The storyteller plays to his or her audience, shortening or lengthening a story as time permits, or simplifying or elaborating it as the age and interest of the audience requires. Nevertheless, the storyteller dares not drastically change the way in which the story unfolds, and certainly not the story's meaning. A story is changeable in its telling, but unchanging in its message. It is in the story's telling that the message is made "new" again, and, thereby, the reputation of a "good" storyteller is confirmed by an audience who has heard it many times before.

The Iroquois have been farmers for about one thousand years, growing corn, beans, and squash, known to them as *The Three Sisters* or *Our Life Supporters*. Despite the importance of farming, the world most frequently described in collections of Iroquois stories is that of the hunter, the fisherman, and the gatherer. Farming never completely replaced the hunting, fishing, and gathering way of life of their ancestors, nor did it displace this way of life as preserved in their stories. Told within the security of home and village, Iroquois stories most frequently tell of the world which lies beyond the surrounding woods-edge and of the other-than-human kinds of people dwelling there.

The Iroquois do not live in a *natural* world, but in a *social* world comprised of real human man-beings, like themselves, and of other kinds of people, or man-beings. These other man-beings are the animal kinds of people and the plant kinds of people, who occasionally take the guise of real human man-beings, but who most frequently appear in their primary animal and plant forms. There are other man-beings, who have as their normal form that of so-called—in our culture—inanimate objects, among them, Mother Earth, Grandmother Moon, Elder Brother Sun, and Grandfather Thunder.

Members of these other-than-human kinds or "tribes" of people are Iroquois kinsmen and kinswomen, addressed as "grandfather," "grandmother," "mother," "uncle," "nephew," "brother," "sister," or "cousin," for example. These terms are not just so many words. They describe the social relations, which exist between real human kinds of people and the other-than-human kinds of people, and the responsibilities each has for the other, as set forth by The Creator. Ceremonies and their rituals fulfill these social contracts.

The Iroquois traditions reprinted here are principally stories about the animal kinds of people, whose appearances, habits, and habitats have contributed to their "typecasting." Color plays an important role in this. For example, white animals possess great powers,

as whiteness symbolizes power; but power which may
be used either for socially constructive or socially de-
constructive purposes. When used beneficially, whiteness is also the color of spiritual, social, and physical
well-being. Animals with black faces or black "masks"
across their eyes, the raccoon preeminent among
them, are frequently cast to play the parts of "trick-
sters" or others who did not live or "play by the rules"
that guide the conduct of others. Long-bodied and
long-tailed animals are endowed with special powers.
The black-tipped white feather of the bald eagle man-
being and the black-tipped white tail of the least weasel man-being, or ermine, have something more in
common, other than just their identically patterned
colors.

Iroquois oral traditions have been recorded since
the early sixteenth century. Recollect and Jesuit mis-
sionaries among the related Huron people of south-
western Ontario were the first to systematically
collect, translate, and publish them, such as within
the seventeenth-century *Jesuit Relations*. Beginning in
the early nineteenth century, Iroquois scholars themselves began to record and publish their oral traditions, David Cusick, a Tuscarora, being the first
among them in 1826 [1848]. Late in the nineteenth
century, another Tuscarora, John N. B. Hewitt, began
a long, distinguished career as an ethnologist for the
Smithsonian Institution, collecting and translating Ir-

oquois myths, legends, and folktales. These were published in numerous·articles and monographs well into the present century, including a collaborative effort with the folklorist Jeremiah Curtin, published in 1918. Arthur C. Parker, a Seneca, published numerous articles and books on the subject beginning in 1908, during his half-century long career as museologist, ethnologist, and archaeologist, first at the New York State Museum and then at the Rochester Museum [and Science Center]. One of his protégés, Jesse Cornplanter, "the Seneca boy artist," published his own collection of stories in 1938.

None of these collections have the charm of Arthur C. Parker's *Skunny Wundy* with its illustrations, prepared by George Armstrong for the edition reprinted here, or by Will Crawford in the original edition. For those who would like to venture deeper into the Iroquois world of real human man-beings and their relations with the other-than-human kinds of people, or who would like to learn more about *Skunny Wundy*'s author, I recommend the following publications:

Cornplanter, Jesse J. *Legends of the Longhouse.* Told to Sah-Nee-Weh, the White Sister [Mrs. Walter A. Hendricks]. Philadelphia: Lippincott, 1938.

Curtin, Jeremiah. *Seneca Indian Myths.* New York: Dutton, 1922.

———, and John N. B. Hewitt. *Seneca Fiction, Legends and Myths.* 32d Annual Report of the Bureau of American Ethnology for the Years 1910–1911. Washington, D.C.: Smithsonian Institution, 1918.

Cusick, David. *Sketches of Ancient History of the Six Nations. Comprising First—A Tale of the Foundation of the Great Island (Now North America,) the Two Infants Born, and the Creation of the Universe. Second—A Real Account of the Early Settlers of North America, and Their Dissensions. Third—Origin of the Kingdom of the Five Nations, Which Was Called A Long House: the Wars, Fierce Animals, &c.* Lockport, N.Y.: Turner and McCollum [printers], 1848.

Fenton, William N. " 'This Island,' the World on the Turtle's Back." *Journal of American Folklore* 75, no. 298 (1962): 283–300.

Fenton, William N., ed. Editor's Introduction. In *Parker on the Iroquois,* 1–47. Syracuse: Syracuse Univ. Press, 1968.

Parker, Arthur C. *Seneca Myths and Legends.* Buffalo Historical Society Publications, vol. 23. Buffalo: Buffalo Historical Society, 1923.

Thomas, W. Stephen. "Arthur Caswell Parker: 1881–1955: Anthropologist, Historian and Museum Pioneer." *Rochester History* 17, no. 3 (1955): 1–20.

Zeller, Terry. "Arthur C. Parker: A Pioneer in American Museums." *Curator* 50, no. 1 (1987): 41–62.

———. "Arthur Parker and the Educational Mission of American Museums." *Curator* 32, no. 2 (1989): 104–22.

SKUNNY WUNDY

From the Introduction
to the First Edition

ONCE UPON A TIME THERE WAS A BIG HOUSE BETWEEN two creeks. It was the home of Planter, one of the chiefs of the Seneca Indian people who lived along the two creeks.

This big house has a lot to do with this book, for in that house lived my grandfather, the chief, and I lived there, too. I was a boy and liked to hear stories about bears and bobcats.

My father was given Deerfoot's Indian name and belonged to the clan of the Tip-Up, while I was given the name of Skoak when I was very small because I jumped around so much. Skoak means Frog. When I grew older, I was taken into the clan of the Bears and given the name of one of their war chiefs. I was called Gawaso Wanneh.

In my grandfather's house there were many relics of the old days. There were war clubs and toma-hawks, bows and arrows, skins of wildcats and bears, and of wolves, too. Hidden away in chests were buckskin garments and moccasins, wampum belts and strings of beads. But these things were put away for memory's sake and long ago have gone to the great museums.

Into that home drifted many a visitor from the wilder parts of the reservation, visitors who lived back in the woods or on the hill where the long-house people dwelt, they who followed the old Indian customs and had grotesque masks and dances and who wore feathers and buckskins.

Many of the Indian visitors stayed for supper and then sat around the fire to smoke. All the youngsters of the family would whisper to Grandfather asking if the visitor would not tell a story. And almost everytime, he would.

There was one thing that may seem odd to you. Every old Indian expected to be called "Uncle," and each always spoke to us as "Nephew." And so it was that as we grew acquainted we would eagerly say, "Uncle, tell us a story."

What fun we had, listening big eyed to the tales of ancient times. There were all kinds of storytellers who told about all kinds of things, from fairies the Seneca Indians call Jung-ga-on, or Jungies, to foxes.

In the old days before the white men came, these stories were told in the great bark houses of the Iroquois Indians—and the Senecas belonged to the Iroquois League.

Of course our Eastern Indians did not live in te-
pees like the Western tribes. Instead they made wonderful houses of posts covered with elm bark. Some of
their houses were two hundred feet long. These Indians, who were my own ancestors, had great planta-
tions in the long-ago days, and they raised vast fields
of corn, beans, squashes, melons, and tobacco. They
had towns and forts, and they had a wise govern-
ment, too.

Hiawatha was an Iroquois, and one of his great
friends who helped him found the Iroquois League
of Peace was Je-gon-sa-seh, a direct descendant of the
woman who came to earth from the sky to become
the first mother of all the Indians. My grandfather's
mother was a direct descendant of this famous woman
known as the Mother of Nations, and so I often heard
about this ancestress and about the true story of
Hiawatha, the lawgiver and wise man, who started
the nations on the pathways of peace.

Of course we knew that winter was the real time
for storytelling and that to tell tales when the grass
was green would bring bees to sting us, bugs to bite
us, and snakes might crawl in our beds. And, as a
matter of fact, the old storytellers never did tell us
old tales except when the frost was in the air. It was
forbidden by ancient custom.

As the years went by, I met many of the famous
tribal storytellers. When I grew up and went to school

far from home, I often sent presents to them so that when I saw them again they would know that I was grateful and so tell me more stories. In this manner, I listened on many a winter's night to the marvelous tales of old Cornplanter, of Big Kettle, and of Dondey and Gawey. I filled many pages with notes and in later years wrote books about Indian stories for students to read.

But after all, these tales are for boys and girls. It is a shame to hide them away. I wouldn't have liked it when I was a boy, so I am going to tell these stories— not in the Indian tongue or even in the exact way that Indians tell them—but in the way boys and girls can understand.

I know I have told these stories right because my father, older and wiser than I, liked the way I have written them. And he knew, for he heard these tales a long time ago in the days of Deerfoot, the swift runner.

—ARTHUR C. PARKER (GAWASO WANNEH)

Skunny Wundy Tricks Old Fox

IN THE DIM LONG AGO, BEFORE RED PEOPLE CAME TO the world, there was a great forest and a mighty river. In this forest were mountains, and in the mountains were mysterious caves, deep and dark.

Here lived great tribes of fur folk, feather folk, thick swarms of bugs and many clans of hippety-hoppers.

In those days all the forest creatures could talk to one another in the same language, but they couldn't sing together at all. Once they tried it, but each had his own tune and there was such a miserable din that Old Man Thunderer made a big rainstorm, and so while it rained he did some tall singing himself.

Nobody liked to have Old Man Thunderer roar out his rumbly song, and so after that all the animals and birds and creepy-crawlers made up their minds to sing songs all by their lonely selves. So that's how *that* happened, and now comes the real story, nephew.

In the first place there was a clever fellow named
Fox. Of course he knew he was clever, which was bad
enough, for everybody knew it too—to his sorrow. In
the second place, Fox was given to bragging most
dreadfully. He was fond of sitting on a mossy hummock and sunning himself while he talked to himself
and anyone else who would listen.

"Oh, you, all of you everywhere," he would begin, "look at me and notice my handsome ways.
Listen to me and learn how clever I am. Oh ho, clever
am I! I can catch any creature whose name I know,
but never a creature catches me, hi ho!"

In those days, as everyone knows, to be a skilled
hunter was the aim of every creature in the big forest,
and the better the hunter the greater was his fame.

Fox was a great hunter, and this didn't set well
in the minds of the furry folk or the feather folk.
After all, who likes to get caught and eaten up? Maybe you, nephew, but not I.

Fine was the day and warm was the sun when
Fox sat on a log beside the river. His fur was fluffy and
red, his tail was fluffy and long. He was highly satisfied
with himself, as foxes have been ever since.

Again he started his boast, "I can catch any creature whose name I know, but never a creature catches
me, hi ho!"

"Who have you caught, I'd like to know?" said a
voice.

Fox looked around in a startled way, for his ears had not detected anyone near.

"Who's talking?" snuffed Fox, blinking his eyes.

"Better-Guess—he's talking," said the voice.

Fox looked sharply and saw a stranger. Who could he be?

"Greeting, Stranger," said Fox with an assumption of merriment.

"Greeting, Fox," said Better-Guess.

"What are you doing here?" inquired Fox, with a wrinkle in his brow.

"Better guess," answered Better-Guess. "That's my name."

" 'Tisn't your real name, though," challenged Fox. "What's your real name?"

"Better-Guess," came the reply. "Now it's my turn to ask questions."

"I might not answer," said Fox, a bit sulkily.

"I think you will," smiled the stranger, who looked mighty clever himself, with his long legs and shaggy head. "For instance, what have you caught?"

"Everything," answered Fox.

"Me?" inquired Better-Guess.

"Well, you're nobody, and I don't know your name. So how could I ever catch you?"

"If I tell you my real name could you catch me?" asked Better-Guess.

"Course I could," laughed Fox. "Go on and tell me for the fun of it, hi ho!" And Fox smiled as he drew his eyes to slits.

"Well, my name is—I suppose you know since you are a clever fellow, hi ho! My name is—why, as I said before, it's Better-Guess."

"So it's Better-Guess, it is?" said Fox, lifting up his nose. "Hmm, hmm! Well I *will* guess, and if I do guess right, what will you give me?"

"All the stories in the world."

"That's fine," replied Fox, "because my real name isn't Fox, you know. Of course you could never guess what my real name is."

"If I do guess," answered Better-Guess, "what will you give me?"

"Same thing," answered Fox. "All the stories in the world, hi ho!"

"I'm ready to have you guess," said Better-Guess. "Four guesses, now."

"Is it Joeagah Waah?" asked Fox.

"No, not Just-like-Raccoon," replied Better-Guess.

"Is it Hum-Stinger?"

"No, not Hornet."

"Is it Whoo-whee?"

"No, not Wind Boy."

"Is it Ga-rhoom?"

"No, not Bullfrog."

"Is it—?"

"You have had your four guesses," said Better-Guess. "You've lost."

"No, do not say that," snarled Fox. "If you guess my name, then you can say I've lost. Come now, guess mine. Remember, four guesses!"

"Is it Silly Braggart?" asked Better-Guess.

"No," growled Fox.

"Is it Turkey-Roost-Robber?"

"No," growled Fox.

"Is it Swagger Tail?"

"No," growled Fox.

"Is it Non-gwat-gwa?"

"How'd you know that?" snarled Fox. "Nobody knows that name except me. But you can't catch me even if you do know it."

"Well, I do win," laughed Better-Guess.

"No, don't say that," begged Fox. "Let me chase you, and if I can't catch you, then you win, hi ho! What do you say?"

"Suits me," said Better-Guess. "How'll we arrange the chase?"

"We'll each get on opposite sides of the river and my task is to catch you. That's how I work," said Fox.

"Suits me," said Better-Guess.

Over the river swam Better-Guess and then the race started, Fox running on one side and Better-Guess on the other.

It was Fox's scheme to cross over on a log and sneak up behind Better-Guess and catch him. But that wasn't Better-Guess's scheme. Oh, no! He kept Fox in sight all the time, but Fox didn't know that.

After awhile Fox came to a thick clump of trees, one of which had fallen across the river, making a bridge. Fox crossed over and began looking for Better-Guess. He ran on until he came to a clearing.

Arrived at the clearing, Fox looked about for his victim. Over the river he heard a voice calling. Fox strained his ears.

"Who are you looking for, Non-gwat-gwa?"

Fox looked, and there on the other side of the stream was Better-Guess.

"I'll catch you yet, Better-Guess!" snapped Fox.

On Fox ran until he came to a place where the river was shallow. Here he crossed with great stealth and concealed himself in a thicket, his nose lifted to catch the scent of Better-Guess. While he sat there, sure that his victim would soon come along, he heard a voice calling.

"Who are you looking for?" came the voice.

Fox gave one startled look and to his disgust saw Better-Guess safe on the other side of the stream.

"How'd you get there?" snapped Fox.

"Better guess!" came the reply, which Fox didn't relish at all.

"I'll catch you yet," growled Fox, as mad as could be.

"Come on," challenged Better-Guess, disappearing down the riverbank.

Fox now began to scheme his wildest schemes, but every time he thought he had Better-Guess cornered, he found to his disappointment Better-Guess was on the opposite side of the stream.

Little did Fox know that the stranger could dive under the water as quickly as an eel and escape every time. Fox only knew that every time he thought he knew just where the stranger was, he was on the opposite bank. Fox was furious at this.

Long did the chase keep up, and a moon waxed and waned before Fox was willing to concede defeat.

From over the river came a voice. "What are you looking for?" it inquired.

"For you," answered Fox truthfully, "but it seems that I never catch you. You are always on the opposite side of the stream."

"Hmm," mused the stranger. "So you admit you are defeated?"

"No, no, don't say that," begged Fox. "Let us only say that when you catch me."

"Suits me," said Better-Guess.

And so Fox began his retreat, skulking here and there and everywhere, crossing and recrossing the stream.

"I've escaped him!" gloated Fox, pausing for breath.

"You have?" inquired a voice behind him. "Why, I've followed your trail from the start." And Better-Guess edged up to Fox with a smile.

Fox gave a great gulp. "I want to say something to you," he said.

There was no answer, and so Fox turned to observe his companion. To his utter amazement, Better-Guess had vanished.

"What are you looking for?" came a voice from over the stream.

"How'd you get there?" panted Fox, now thoroughly frightened.

"Better guess," came the answer. "Hadn't we better say you've lost out?"

"I suppose so," gasped Fox, hiding his face in his paws and crouching down in despair.

"Then start telling me your stories," commanded Better-Guess.

Fox looked up, and there sat Better-Guess at his side.

"All right," answered Fox. "I'll tell you all my stories."

"Tell 'em true," commanded Better-Guess. "Tell everything you've done and seen and tell all the wicked things you've done. I command you!"

"I will," answered Fox. "But before I begin, there is one thing I would like to know. I never will catch you, that's certain, and so there is no harm in my asking."

"Go ahead and ask," came the answer.

"You say your name is Better-Guess," commenced Fox. "Now then, I *will* guess, and if I'm right I'm right."

"Go ahead," was the reply.

"Well, your name isn't Better-Guess, it's Skunny Wundy, and it means Cross-the-Creek," said Fox.

"Well, you *are* a fox," was the answer. "Yes, my name is Skunny Wundy, and I never get caught. Now go on with your stories."

And so every night for a moon Fox told Skunny Wundy his tales, and Skunny Wundy put them all in a bag made of otter skin and hid it away for boys and girls to find when they came on the earth. So that's how we know what the animals used to do in the dim long ago before people came to this old world.

Skunny Wundy—who was he? Well, nephew, you'd better guess too!

Nobody ever saw the first Skunny Wundy except the animals, but since his time there have been a lot of Skunny Wundys.

Mighty hunters are called Skunny Wundy, good storytellers are called Skunny Wundy. Brave boys are called Skunny Wundy, and it's lucky too, because when anything bad happens, they're always "cross the creek."

The stories—ah, yes, the stories old Fox told, well, well. Open your ears, listen, give attention, and you shall hear the wonderful tales Skunny Wundy heard when old Fox told all about his tricks. Listen, for it was I, maybe, who found the otter-skin bag. Na ho!

How Fox and Raccoon
Tricked One Another

IT IS SAID BY THE WISE MEN OF OLD, MY NEPHEW, that Non-gwat-gwa, the Fox, and Joeagah, the Raccoon, once played tricks on each other which made them enemies for life. It was all an affair over swapping hum-houses and fire balls, and it ended in Raccoon making his home in the treetops.

Fox was walking down the woodland trail one warm summer day. He was feeling in good humor because a plump grouse had gone down his throat.

"Now, then," said he, "I would be perfectly satisfied if I had one of those rare magic pawpaws to eat!"

Now it must be explained that in those days before the great era of Man, all animals ate what they pleased, and each knew there were magical things that, once eaten, would make them great hunters. Fox knew there was a wonder bush on which grew magic pawpaws. Should a fox eat one, it would render him invisible.

Thinking how fine it would be to become an invisible hunter, Fox ran down the trail. Suddenly he paused, for there, hanging on a low bush, was something shaped like a turnip. Fox ran around in a circle and then nosed up to the thing. It was gray and queer, and had a thin wall with a hum inside it.

Fox looked shrewdly at this hum-house, and with blinking eyes watched the hum-stingers fly in and out of the little round door at the bottom of their house. Fox had a good idea. When all the hornets had gone inside to sing, he stuck a wad of clay over the door opening and then picked the hum-house off the bush.

"Yak, yak!" thought he, "I now have something fine to trade for pawpaws when I meet some blunderhead fruit picker."

Fox was happy and scampered through the tall grass, through the swamp, and then up by the wood's edge where the bushes grew.

He began to nose around among the big trees until he saw a round black hole between two gnarled roots. He knew that this was the doorway to Joeagah, the raccoon. He also knew that Joeagah was a clever fellow who ought to be trimmed good and proper, for Joeagah was not only smart but knew it, which is a sin, even in the animal world.

To attract attention, Fox began to laugh. "Ho ho, ho ho," he laughed. "Here am I! Know ye I have a treasure I will trade for a treasure. If any man trades me, he'll win magic hum-house."

So saying, Fox trotted away to a mossy hillock and waited, well knowing that every fur and feather brother knew his voice.

Down in the black hole beneath the tree of gnarled roots was Joeagah, the raccoon, looking for adventure in the dark tunnels under the ground. Raccoon was a curious explorer and had felt of everything in the woods except a certain gray thing with a hum inside. Raccoon wanted that hum-house, but as yet he had nothing to trade for it.

Raccoon crawled out his back door like a run-
away woodchuck and crept cautiously to the swamp,
where he pulled up the root of the Jack-in-the-Pulpit,
which the old folk always called *fire ball*.

Raccoon took the fire ball and rolled it in yellow
mud to make it look like a delicious fruit. He rolled it
and rolled it until it was dry, for Raccoon was clever
with his hands and liked to roll things. He then took
the yellow-coated fire ball under his arm and saun-
tered down the trail, making believe that he didn't
know that anyone was about.

Coming to a mossy hillock where the ferns grew
tall, he began to laugh.

"Ho ho, ho ho!" he laughed. "Here am I! Know
ye that I have treasure I will trade for a treasure. If
any man trades me, he'll win magic seedpod."

Out from his hiding place stepped Fox, his eyes
aglitter and his teeth showing white through his
affable smile.

"Good morning," said Fox.

"Good morning," returned Raccoon.

"Where are you going?" inquired Fox.

"Somewhere," answered Raccoon. "Where are
you going?"

"Somewhere," replied Fox. "What have you
there?"

"Something," answered Raccoon. "What have
you there?"

"Something," replied Fox. "What are you going to do with yours?"

"Swap it," answered Raccoon. "What're you going to do with yours?"

"Swap it," replied Fox. "What'll you give me for mine?"

"I don't know," answered Raccoon. "What'll you give for mine?"

"I don't know," replied Fox. "What is the name of your treasure?"

"Better guess," answered Raccoon. "What is the name of your treasure?"

"Better guess," replied Fox. "Come, let's swap."

Raccoon looked at the gray thing with the hum inside and inquired, "Is your treasure the magic bottle with hum inside?"

"Goodness, how you can guess!" exclaimed Fox. "How did you know that I had the magic bottle with hum inside? Why, it is worth so much I never did dare tell anyone I had it, because he who owns it will become the greatest hunter in the whole world."

"I'll swap for that poor thing if you can guess what I have," said Raccoon.

Fox looked at the yellow thing and then inquired, "Is your treasure the magic pawpaw?"

"Goodness, how you can guess!" exclaimed Raccoon. "How did you know that I had the magic pawpaw? Why, it is worth so much that I never dared tell anyone I had it, because he who eats it will become invisible and turn into the greatest hunter in the whole green world."

"All right, let's swap," said Fox, with his eyes blinking and his tongue hanging out with eagerness.

So they swapped, and each went away with his prize, both well pleased.

Pretty soon Raccoon looked at his gray bottle and began to wonder about it. He picked away at the clay stopper of the door. In an eye wink the stopper came out—and with it the whole tribe of hum-stingers! The hum-stingers gave one look and then dashed at Raccoon, stinging him all around his eyes and all over, especially all around his tail.

Oh, how he did fight those hornets! He slew hundreds of them *after* they had stung him, but none before.

Raccoon roared and chattered and scolded and cried like a puppy with a pinched tail. Oh, how he did cry, but then who could help it when a thousand hornets had revenged themselves by sticking in their hot needles?

Weeping and wailing, Raccoon staggered down to the swamp, where he buried himself in the black mud, the best pain plaster in the world. But the stings hurt terribly, especially since Raccoon could hear Fox laughing himself sick over his plight. Oh, how mad this made Raccoon!

After awhile, Fox began to wonder about his treasure and to think how he might eat it and become an unseen hunter of ducks. He looked at the yellow thing and rolled it over on the ground. It was queer shaped for a pawpaw, but then maybe *magic* pawpaws did look queer. He opened his mouth and grabbed the yellow thing. He gave a crushing bite, so eager was he, and then began to chew. He stiffened all over!

Something had happened! With a long, sharp yelp Fox began to caper. Horror of horrors! He had bitten into a fire ball, the most peppery of all forest roots. His tongue burned, his throat burned, and his whole mouth was afire with blistering pain. Down to the swamp he ran to lap up mud to cool his fiery agony.

"Yep, yep," he barked. "If I ever catch that mean, wicked Joeagah, I will eat him alive!"

Raccoon, from his safe hiding place, stuck out one ear. With mighty satisfaction he listened to the howling of Fox and then to his whimpering when his mouth was full of mud. The agony of Fox was cooling medicine to Raccoon. How he did enjoy his revenge. It served Fox right!

After a time Raccoon slipped out of the muck and sought refuge in a treetop, for he well knew that Fox would soon be at his underground cabin door.

Up and up climbed Raccoon until he found a

bed in an old hawk's nest. Here he slept, and many times as he snoozed he laughed at the thought of Fox's suffering.

Little did he know that Fox, in the heat of rage, waited below with his mouth open over the underground door.

When Raccoon had finished his nap, he rubbed his eyes and started down the tree. He wanted a few fat grubs before he went to bed again. But just as he reached the ground, Fox spied him and gave a great leap. But Raccoon was agile and ran back to the tree and scampered up to a big branch, where he peered down at Fox.

"You cheated me, you black faced ring-around-his-tail!" yelped Fox.

"You cheated me, you red shirted can't-climb-a-tree," scolded Raccoon.

"I'll eat you if I catch you," yelped Fox.

"Yes, if you ever catch me," scolded Raccoon. "But no longer do I live in a hole in the ground like you. I live in a tree. Come on up!"

And so, my nephew, the two fought back and forth until Raccoon grew sleepy and Fox grew hungry and slunk away after more partridges.

Since that day the two have never been friends, and Fox hates fire balls as much as Raccoon hates hum-houses that grow on trees. So the old folk say, and this is all they said. Na ho!

Raccoon and
the Three Roasting Geese

WHO SHALL SAY THAT FOX IS NOT ANGRY WHEN tricked? No wise man would say that.

It so happened that Fox was angry at Raccoon for cheating him in a swapping match which made Fox vow to get even. Well, Fox got even, all right, and Raccoon never forgot it either. That's what this story is about.

Fox stuck his slim nose through the grass which grew thick by the river's edge. His black, glinting eyes saw a ball of fur crouching on a rock that rested in the river. "So Raccoon is here," thought Fox. "I'll see what he is up to."

Raccoon very slyly stuck out a paw and grabbed a fine fat goose, wringing its neck. He waited, and along came another goose which he treated in the same manner. Forty eye winks later he caught another goose, and then exclaimed, "Ne-yoh!" which meant he had caught enough.

With great skill Raccoon dragged the geese to the shore and plucked them, laughing as he did, "Oh, hon-gaks make a fine dinner!"

Raccoon built a roaring fire of oak logs. When the flames had turned the wood to embers, he raked them aside, making a pit into which he thrust the three geese, side by side. He heaped the ashes over them, then the glowing coals, and then more ashes until he had a mound with three pairs of feet sticking above it—one and two, three and four, five and six.

Raccoon was now tired and sleepy. It was no easy thing to do all that work. He curled up to go to sleep, but just as he grew comfortable he had a terribly disturbing thought. He leaped up.

"Suppose Fox should smell the smoke and sneak up to find what it was all about? Suppose Fox should smell the roasting geese and steal them?" So thought Raccoon.

He scratched his head, rubbed his face, and licked his paw, all to get an idea. In a bit he got it.

"Ha, ha! I'll scatter ashes all around, and if Fox comes while I am asleep, his tracks will appear," said Raccoon.

"Raa-ux, raa-ux, raa-ux," said something.

Raccoon looked up with a start. "What's that?" he whistled. Then he began to laugh. It was only two beech limbs, pressing together and squeaking when the wind blew.

Little did Raccoon know that Fox had asked Flying Head, the Wind Boy, to blow just a little and make the limbs rub together.

"Say, you limbs up there," exclaimed Raccoon, "do me a favor! If Fox comes about while I am asleep, make a big squeak and wake me up."

"Do-o-gex, do-o-gex," creaked the limbs, which made Raccoon think they answered, "Truly I will." He was satisfied.

"That's good of you," called back Raccoon. "I am going to sleep now. Ho ho, you watch, I'll sleep!"

Raccoon curled up and dreamed a long, hungry dream about a big feast of geese. Fast asleep was he and in the land of dreamers.

This was Fox's chance to sneak around. It was not long before he came. First he cast an acorn at the sleeper, but could not stir him. Next he cast a pebble, but the sleeper did not move. Next he spoke right out loud, "Hi, there, I am going to eat your geese!"

Not a move did the sleeper make.

Fox chuckled softly and began to pull out the roasted geese. Um, um! They were roasted in a delicious manner. Fox ate and ate until he had eaten them all.

Of course the bones and the feet were left, and these Fox carefully buried in the embers, sticking the feet in the ashes, just as they had been in the first place.

Fox now felt highly pleased with himself and
began to dance all around, for he saw the ashes and
wanted to make tracks. He knew Raccoon would be
terribly mad when he saw them. Ho ho!

After awhile Fox felt sick because he had eaten
so much and he slunk away to rest up a bit. Of course
he didn't go far. He just sneaked back of the tree
where he could watch Raccoon.

"Wind Boy, up there, make a noise," said Fox
softly.

Wind Boy blew a little, and the trees creaked,
"Djoe-a-gah, djoe-a-gah!" This was Raccoon's name
and he awoke with great suddenness. Up he jumped
and looked around.

Savory smells sizzled out of the roasting mound.
"The geese are done," thought Raccoon. "Hmm," he
mumbled, "now for the feast."

He pulled up the first leg and it was just a bone.
He pulled up the second leg and it was just a bone.
So was the third leg and the fourth. Again he pulled
at the legs, but the fifth leg and sixth were just bones,
and no goose came with them.

Raccoon was now in a great rage.

Disregarding all caution, he flew at the embers
and raked them away, burning his fur and scorching
his face—traces of which can be seen to this day.
Down in the bottom of the ember heap he discovered
some bones, all picked neatly of their meat.

Raccoon looked around the fire and saw the tracks of Fox.

"Thieving trickster!" screamed Raccoon. "Dirty scoundrel, he has stolen my geese! I'll fix the red-headed quail-hunter!"

He ran around and around looking for signs of Fox, but could not tell where his enemy had gone.

Little did he know that Fox was looking through the weeds and holding his mouth shut with his paws to keep from laughing right out loud.

"I know what I'll do first," said Raccoon to himself. "I'll punish those limbs for not telling me."

He looked up at the offending branches. "Say, you limbs," scolded Raccoon, "why didn't you make a noise and wake me up? You're no good, you drab-coated sticks. I'm coming up to bite you."

"Saa-nee-haa, saa-nee-haa," creaked the limbs, which made Raccoon think they were calling out, "Don't do that!"

So Raccoon scampered up the tree and ran to the crossed limbs which squeaked. He stood on both of them and then lifted his paw to strike the spot where they crossed each other. Down went his paw with a terrible stroke. Apart flew the limbs and then together again with a quick snap. Wind Boy had done the trick—he, the mischief-friend of Fox.

"Oh, oh!" squealed Raccoon. "Let go! I didn't know you could bite! You've caught my paw."

Raccoon struggled until he lost his balance and fell off the branches and swung high in the air.

"Whee, whee," he screamed. "Let go, let go!"

Fox looked up with great interest, but he could not laugh. He had such a terrible ache inside. Those three geese were picking away so savagely inside him —he was sorry he had eaten all of them now.

Raccoon kept on squealing in such a comical fashion that Fox, in spite of his pain, couldn't help but creep out to enjoy his enemy's discomfort.

"Hi, you, up there!" called out Fox. "What are you doing in that tree swinging by one paw?"

"Oh, get me down," begged Raccoon.

"Why should I help you, cousin?" asked Fox. "You deserve all you are getting. Remember the time you fed me fire ball and burned my throat out?"

"Oh, get me down," begged Raccoon.

"Why should I get you down?" laughed Fox as best he could, for those geese were making trouble inside. "Remember the time you called me names?"

"Oh, get me down," begged Raccoon. "I will forgive you for eating my geese. I won't hold it against you."

"Well, I hold it against you, all right," said Fox, rubbing his tummy. "You can't cook anything fit to eat."

"Oh, get me down," squealed Raccoon. "I'll give anything to get down."

"What will you give?" inquired Fox.

"All the geese in the world," replied Raccoon. "You can eat them all after this. Besides, if you let me down I'll tell you something you ought to know to save your life."

"Save my life?" echoed Fox, doubling up with pain. "What do you mean? I'm not going to die, am I?"

"Yes, you are going to die unless I help you," answered Raccoon.

Fox twisted up into a knot of torment. What a stomachache he had!

"All right," said Fox, as soon as he could speak. "I'll ask Wind Boy to blow a little and let you down."

Of course Wind Boy obeyed Fox and moved the tree just enough to loosen Raccoon's poor pinched paw. Down he fell with a thud which nearly knocked the breath out of him.

"Oh, Fox, oh, Fox!" was all he could say.

"Well, what were you going to tell me?" inquired Fox, doubling up again with pain.

"You're poisoned!" exclaimed Raccoon. "I put poison in those geese because I was afraid Wolverine would find them while I slept."

"Poison?" yelped Fox. "What kind of poison?"

"Fox poison," asserted Raccoon, licking his sore paw. "It is the worst kind, and I knew if it would kill foxes it would kill wolverines."

"Then you weren't going to eat those geese?" yelped Fox, with a ghastly look on his face.

"No," lied Raccoon. "I was trying to revenge myself on the meanest fellow I know."

"Oh, oh," groaned Fox, rubbing his tummy.

"Oh, oh," groaned Raccoon, sucking his poor pinched paw.

"What'll I do?" inquired Fox.

"Get medicine," answered Raccoon.

"Who from?"

"From me."

"You got some?"

"Yes."

"Give me some."

"What'll you give for a dose?"

"What do you want?"

"Three well-roasted geese."

"All right, I'll get 'em. Give me the medicine."

"Chew up these six gristly feet and call yourself names," commanded Raccoon. "That's the medicine."

Fox chewed up the feet and called himself all the terrible names he could think of. "I'm a mud-mouth, I'm a mud puppy, I'm a split-lip, I'm a hippety-hopper, I'm a mean-hummer!" he shouted.

"Now get the geese and roast them," commanded Raccoon. "Quick now, I'm hungry."

So Fox caught the geese and fixed them for the

roast. Then he went down to the river and chewed calamus root. After that he felt better.

"Hmm," Fox thought, "I wonder if Raccoon was fooling me. I'll bet he was just making me chew feet and call myself names to get revenged. Oh, I'll fix him!"

Fox felt a lot better now and so he watched the geese roast. The calamus roots stopped his inside aching and his mind became sharper, but still he pretended to be terribly sick.

"Oh, I am so sick yet," he howled. "Those gristly feet make me sicker than ever. I'm afraid I'll die. Don't go to sleep, cousin," he pleaded.

"Guess I will curl up and sleep," said Raccoon. "You watch those geese or you'll surely die. Remember, I haven't given you the final cure yet."

So saying, Raccoon ran up the tree and curled up on a big limb right over the fire. Looking down with one open eye, he saw the feet of the geese—one, two, three, four, five, six. As he closed his eye, he smelled the savory odors of the cooking geese. Then he fell into a deep slumber.

Fox wanted no more geese, but just for a frolic he opened the ashes enough to let out the most appetizing odors that ever steamed from an ash-oven. Delicious!

Whispering to Wind Boy, he said, "Blow this smell to Wolverine."

Wind Boy did just as he was told, and soon Wolverine came trotting along.

"Get out," snorted Wolverine. "Where I come, everyone else leaves the scene."

Fox ran around the tree and waited as Wolverine, the glutton, ate the geese, feet and all, and then departed.

After awhile Raccoon awoke and, smelling the remains of the feast, scrambled down from his perch. He looked with angry eyes at the scattered ashes.

"Where are my geese?" he demanded, with fire in his eyes and his teeth parted.

"Your geese?" yelped back Fox. "Your geese? Why, you gave me all the geese in the world as the price of your release from the pinch of those limbs up there, so when the geese were done I ate them."

"You ate them!" screamed Raccoon. "Why, I thought you had eaten enough goose to be sick!"

"Well, I got over it," answered Fox.

"But I cured you," snapped Raccoon.

"Like fun, you did," laughed Fox. "Calamus root cured me."

Raccoon was now as mad as a mean-hummer. "Go away!" he snarled. "For one thing, you think you've starved me, but you haven't."

"Ah, me," sighed Fox, "if you are sorry I saved your life, I'll go. But I am as mad as can be that I didn't leave you hanging in the tree. It would have served you right, because you can't learn anything."

"What can't I learn?" snapped Raccoon.

"You can't learn to keep awake when your meat is on the fire," answered Fox. "But that isn't all you can't learn."

"What else can't I learn?" inquired Raccoon, greatly vexed.

"That you should never ask for what you have given away," answered Fox, swishing his tail and sauntering down the trail.

Raccoon scowled as he watched the retreating form of the old red fox. "It is a hard fate," thought he, "to be in debt to an enemy, especially if he be a clever fellow."

Thereupon he fell to cracking goose bones and licking out the marrow. "He can't starve me," growled Raccoon. "Little does he know that the best part of the meat lies in the heart of the bones."

So this is what the old folk say, and it must be true. Na ho!

How the Wood Duck
Got His Red Eyes
and Sojy Had His Coat Spoiled

Yo ho, nephew! Ducks, ducks, all kinds of ducks!

Long ago, before there were any human people in the world, it was full of ducks—all kinds of ducks, but they were all one color.

There was one creature who looked like a man, but wasn't a man. He had a good red coat which had a long fluffy tail like a gray squirrel, but he wasn't a gray squirrel. Oh, no, he was much bigger and had pointed ears and a long narrow nose.

Can you guess who he was? Well, anyway, he was known as Mischief Maker, but wise old folk in their language called him S'hojiosko. We'll call him Sojy for short.

Well, Sojy was taking a walk one day. It was a fine morning. The first thing he knew, he came to a small pool of water where an old man was painting leaves. Oh, he was putting pretty colors on the leaves!

Sojy stopped short and looked at him. He had an idea
to have some fun.

"Hi, old man," he called. "It's a fine morning!"

"I knew that before," called out the old man.

"What sort of a thing are you doing there?"
asked Sojy, a bit peeved.

"Oh, just minding my own business!" answered
the old man.

"Well, you are not, old mud puppy," snapped
Sojy.

"Well, it certainly isn't *your* business," replied
the old man.

"Oh ho, somebody thinks he is wise," said Sojy.
"You think you can paint leaves, but you can't. I see
one you can't paint."

"Ho, ho, ho!" laughed the old man. "I have
been painting leaves ever since the world began.
Don't you know who I am? I'm Autumn."

This made Sojy think hard. He was very foxy
and could get up sly schemes. After awhile he said,
"I see a leaf way down in that water. Look in and
see if you can paint it."

So saying, Sojy held out a twig with one leaf and
let it reflect in the water.

Autumn looked in and saw the leaf. With a dash
of his brush he hit at the leaf, but he could not touch
it. The water only washed away his colors. This made
Sojy, the mischief maker, laugh long and loud.

"Well, good-bye, Old Man Autumn," he called out. "When you can paint that leaf, I will let you wipe your brushes on me. I'll come around tomorrow to see if *you* are minding *your* own business."

Old Man Autumn was stumped. Ho ho, he was stumped!

Sojy went walking along and came to the shore of a big lake where there were many cattail reeds. He heard a great fuss there and, creeping near, saw a big flock of ducks. He was hungry and was fond of ducks. What good fortune!

"I'm terribly hungry," said he to himself, "but I can't swim out after ducks. What will I do? Ho ho, I have it!"

So saying, he ran up on the shore and sat on a little mound. "Good morning, everybody!" he called out. "Say, it's a fine morning for folk like you."

The ducks all looked up in surprise, for they knew that Sojy had an appetite for them. They were not going to be fooled, however. No, no, no—not *those* ducks.

"Quack, quack, honk, honk!" they laughed.

"I was just going to say that you were quite hoarse for such a nice morning," said Sojy. "You ought to improve your voices. What a rough noise you make when you talk. All kinds of birds can sing, but all you sing is 'quack, quack, honk, honk.' Now, I have a magic song. Just listen to me."

Sojy opened his wide mouth, rolled his eyes, and sang:

Fair is my voice, how I can sing, can sing!
I learned it all by just dancing, dancing!
Who dances now, no matter who, who-oo, who-oo!
Oh, he can sing, and warble too, too-oo, too-oo!

The ducks looked up and one said, "Honk, honk! This fellow seems fair enough and wants to teach us how to sing. Come on, let us find out how it is done, we're safe enough."

"What shall we do?" called out Mallard.

"Oh, just come ashore awhile and build a house of cattails I can't get through. Then while it is dark inside, try to sing and dance. Outside I will sing, too, and when I have finished, you will have as sweet voices as ever came out of the sky."

"Anything else?" asked Wood Duck, very suspiciously.

"Well, only just this," answered Sojy. "When magic is being done you must keep your eyes shut tight—just as tight as the bark on a tree. Don't you dare open them or you will lose your voices and your eyes will turn as red as blood. Don't open your eyes!"

"Thought so," answered Wood Duck. "I guess we will swim out in the lake a bit further. Yes, yes."

"No, no," quacked the other ducks. "We are all going to dance and gain fine, sweet voices."

So the chief duck ordered them ashore and they built a round, bowl-like house of cattail reeds and then all went inside.

"Quack hard and dance hard," called out Sojy. "I will sing the magic song, but you must not hear a word or a sound of it. If you do, you will all turn to

stones. Just keep dancing and make all the noise you
can. After awhile you will get sweet little voices, just
sweet enough for the world in the sky where strawberries grow the year around. Ho ho!"

So the ducks began a wild dance, honking like
forty geese fighting over a bowl of mush. How they
did quack and honk!

Pretty soon Sojy stuck his long furry arm in the
peek hole by the door and grabbed a fat duck by
the neck. It could not quack anymore, so tightly did
Sojy hold on. He drew it forth and wrung its neck.
Again and again he thrust his arm into the house
and drew forth a duck. Soon he had a big pile of
ducks. The honking inside quite naturally grew less
and less.

Now Wood Duck was inside, but he wasn't very
sure that all was well. So when he felt something
slide by him, he opened his eyes and saw Sojy's arm
grabbing Bufflehead.

"He's killing us, he's killing us!" quacked out
Wood Duck.

At that, the ducks all began to flutter and tried
to open their eyes, but they couldn't, so tightly had
they kept them shut.

Only Wood Duck had his eyes open. Ho, ho, 'tis
a good thing to keep your eyes open even when you
sleep, nephew—you listening?

Up the ducks flew right against the top of their

house, and up they flew until they lifted the house clear of the ground and into the sky.

All the while, Wood Duck kept calling, "It's enough, it's enough!"

After awhile the ducks heard him, and down they came, house and all. Ho ho! Down came the house, and down it came until it was right over the pond of Old Man Autumn. The house fitted right over the old man, pond and all. And there they all were in the dark, ho ho!

Pretty soon Old Man Autumn said, "Whew, it got dark all of a sudden. I wonder why all those ducks are here."

The ducks on being spoken to were able to reply.

Wood Duck told the story and said that except for him, all the others were blind.

"Too bad," answered Old Man Autumn. Then he said to all the ducks, "Tell you what I'll do. I will open your eyes for you if you'll do me a favor. That old trickster Sojy fooled me, too. He says I can't paint a leaf's reflection in the water. If I do, he says, he will let me wipe my brushes on him.

"Now one of you must dive down with a painted leaf, and when Sojy holds the green one over the water, the fellow under the water must hold out the painted leaf. When Sojy looks in the water, he will see it. Then you just watch me! I'll have all kinds of things chase Sojy."

"We all agree," honked out the ducks. So Old Man Autumn had the ducks soak their heads in his pool for a few moments and then he rubbed ginseng seeds on them. Open popped their eyes.

Then the ducks tore down their reed house and flung the cattails all around the pool.

Old Man Autumn painted a leaf and gave it to Coot, who showed how he could dive and stay under water as long as a frog. The ducks now hid.

Along came Sojy, swinging along as if he were quite a big fellow. "Morning, Old Man Autumn," he said. "I've come to see if you can paint that leaf, ho ho!"

He held a leaf over the pool and Old Man Autumn, looking in, began to mix his colors. Soon Old Man stuck his brush in the water and then, pop! out came the leaf in the water as red and yellow as any on the trees. Coot had done the trick properly.

Sojy was dumbfounded and commenced to say, "Well, I didn't think—I didn't know—I didn't—"

But Autumn answered, "Just as smart fellows so often do!"

"Guess I'll be going now—you win this contest, Old Man," said Sojy.

"Wait a bit, wait a bit!" called out Old Man Autumn. "We have a bargain. I am going to wipe my brushes on you, Sojy. You have done enough mischief!"

"No, no, no—please, not this time! I was only fooling," begged Sojy.

"Well, I am not," answered Old Man Autumn, mixing some clay from his pool and smearing it all over Sojy's chest and leggings. He looked at the gray shirt front and then wiped some of his charcoal down the back of Sojy's red coat. It was enough.

Sojy yelped and cried and rolled over and tried to wipe the color off, but he couldn't. The stains stayed, and the pure red suit was all gone. It was marked with gray and black.

Sojy was much ashamed, especially when the ducks swam out from the reeds and began to quack.

"I don't care," he yelped. "That Wood Duck fellow has red eyes anyway and can't change them now."

"I don't care," quacked Wood Duck. "You're fixed so you'll be chased and hunted and stalked by all sorts of animals now, you mischief maker!"

At that, Coot came up with the painted leaf in his bill, and at that a pack of hungry dogs came out of the bushes and chased Sojy into a hole.

Ho ho, nephew! Now you know how Wood Duck got red eyes, and so suspicious is he that he now builds his nest in a tree. But I bet you can't guess who Sojy turned out to be. Ho ho! Maybe you can, but so that you won't be wrong, I'll tell you his name is also Bushy Tail. That's all, nephew.

Wink, the Lazy Bird, and the Red Fox

THE OLD FOLK SAY THAT THERE WAS ONCE A LAZY
bird called Chewink—Wink for short. It may be true,
nephew, that he was lazy, but Wink said it wasn't
that at all. He said that he was only tired all the time
and didn't like to do anything.

And so the old story goes that Wink was so lazy
that he didn't hunt corn grubs like other Chewink
boys, nor would he gather seed or pick buds. This
was too bad, my nephew, as I shall tell. So now the
story, ho ho, the story!

Once, upon a hill by the banks of the Djo-nes-
see-yu, there was a lonely cabin built of straw and
leaves. Here lived Oneta and her only son, Wink.
Oneta was a widow whose husband and four babes
had been killed in the war raid of the hawk tribe—
those terrible Gajidas warriors that swoop down
from the blue! So, naturally, Wink had no father to
bring him up. Poor boy, he had nothing to do but eat

the meals his mother prepared and sleep the rest of the day.

After awhile his mother scolded him roundly, saying that he was a lazy loafer and should do a little hunting for himself now and then. They had not had fresh meat since that day when Oneta picked fish out of the mud holes after the river had gone down.

Wink couldn't stand being scolded twice a day. One morning when he had been sent for water, he crawled into his mother's canoe and floated downstream. After awhile the canoe struck a log jutting from the shore, and Wink, being too tired after his journey to push it off again, crawled ashore. He found a mossy bank under a basswood tree with fine, sweet smelling flowers.

Here Wink lay all day, making a miserable meal from artichokes the river had washed out.

Poor boy, how was he to get home again? The stream was swift, and to return meant he would have to paddle upstream against the swift current. Wink, of course, could not do that, for he was too tired.

As he lay pondering over his misfortune, for night was coming on, he heard a voice. Without looking up, Wink replied, "Kwey! What do you want? Can't you see I'm busy?"

"I want to borrow your canoe to paddle upstream," said the voice.

"All right," answered the lucky Wink. "You

can borrow it if you will take me up to the flats at
Gardow."

The stranger now came into sight, and a fine
looking fellow was he with a coat of long red fur and
a big bushy tail.

"Come on," he exclaimed with a smile. "Come
on, for I just like to paddle for other people, especially—well, especially. . . ." And somehow he didn't
finish, but placed a covered basket in the bow of the
canoe.

So Wink went home. His face was long and de-
jected, for he had not even killed a beetle that day
and was compelled to eat dried meat for supper. It
was a terrible task to chew it, but it was the best his
mother could borrow from over the hill.

Next day he floated downstream again, and that
evening the same stranger came along and wanted to
borrow the canoe. Of course Wink agreed if the
stranger would do the paddling.

In this manner for many moons Wink escaped
scoldings and secured his much needed rest.

After a time, Wink began to notice the stranger
was lugging a heavy basket. Each night he stowed
it away with care in the bow of the canoe. One night
he asked the stranger what was in it.

"Oh, the basket? Basket—oh, yes. Hmm. Why
it's full of treasure I dig from the ground near the
spot where you sleep all day."

"What sort of treasure is it?" asked Wink.

"Oh, just wonderful treasure that belongs to a boy named Wink, but he doesn't want it. It is a treasure of Kan-yenga, of Onoh, and of Owis-ha, and it all belongs to a boy named Wink. Ho ho!"

"Why, my name is Wink," said the lazy boy.

"Oh, no, that cannot be," replied the red stranger. "No boy like Wink would lie all day and sleep and let a stranger steal his treasure from the ground at his feet. If you were Wink, you would have dug for the treasure."

"But my name is Wink and the treasure is mine," persisted Wink. "Give me all you have dug."

"Not I," said the stranger. "I'd rather eat you first."

Wink was now frightened a bit, for he noticed the stranger had a big, hungry mouth. So he said with a little more humility, "Please give me what is left of the treasure. I must have it."

"All right," answered the red stranger. "The last of the treasure is a message from the Jungie that

guarded it. He spoke and said, 'All the treasures of
Kan-yenga and Onoh and Owis-ha are Wink's. It
is all buried in a place known as I-wonder-where-it-
is-now. It is there beneath a little earth.' And what
Jungie said I repeat," he concluded, looking at Wink.

Wink was very angry someone else had taken
his treasure, but he hid his anger and asked, "How
shall I get back my treasure?"

"Dig for it here, and dig for it there," said the
red stranger. "Dig by the river, by the hill, by the
wood's edge, by the field's edge. Dig every day, for
what you find is priceless to you."

Wink was now fired with a new ambition, and
every day he dug here and he dug there, by the river,
by the hill, by the wood's edge, and by the field's edge.

All the birds came around to see him dig, and
the birds thought Wink their best friend, for where
he dug the worms came out and the birds grew fat
from the worms. Moreover, where Wink dug, Oneta,
his mother, planted corn, so there was food to eat.

After awhile, the birds began to disappear one
by one, and Wink thought he saw old Red Fox
skipping here and there, each time with a quail or
partridge.

Wink resolved to watch for Fox and follow him
into the woods to find what treasure he had concealed
in his den.

Wink crept cautiously into the woods and along

a ridge of rock, where he found the lair of old Red
Fox. He looked carefully and saw that Red Fox was
none other than the stranger who had borrowed his
canoe.

Wink crouched down in the leaves and listened.
Someone was singing:

Wink digs here and Wink digs there,
Wink digs almost everywhere.
And where Wink digs, the worms all come,
Where worms all come, the birds all come,
Where birds all come, that's where I come.
Hi ho hum! Yum, yum, yum!

Up in the top of a tall maple a wheezy voice
spoke. "What do you mean by that song, old Red
Fox?" asked the voice. "You sing that every night as
you chuckle over your thrush meat and turkey."

It was Flying Head, the mischievous Wind Boy,
speaking.

Up spoke Red Fox. "Ho, ho ho!" he roared. "It
is all very funny indeed. Early this spring I met a lazy
boy named Wink who allowed me to paddle him
home in his canoe. I told him I had found a treasure
belonging to him and had buried it again. He wanted
it, so I told him to dig for it by the river, by the hill,
by the wood's edge, and by the field's edge. Everywhere he digs, the worms all come. And where the
worms all come, the birds all come, and where the

birds all come, there I come—and grab 'em for my
supper. This is the way lazy Wink pays me for
paddling him home."

Wink heard every word and bit his lip as he
crept back to the spot where he had been digging.

"So there is treasure after all," he mused, as he
grabbed his stone hoe and dug like mad. He was now
bound to dig everywhere until he had found all the
treasure that had been buried, for was it not his?

Long did he dig until he made a vast clearing
where his old mother planted corn and pumpkins
and harvested large crops. Wide and fertile were her
fields, and from many lands hunters and traders came
for her harvest. How proud she was of her boy Wink,
who dug so many fields for her.

"I believe Wink is the busiest fellow alive," said
the mother to a group of hunters who came for corn.
"If he had not cleared so many fields and dug them
for planting, we should not have this corn, these
beans, and these pumpkins. Our storehouses are full,
and we have vast treasure indeed. Wink made all this
possible."

Over in the woods while she praised her boy, a
red-coated stranger picked feathers from his teeth
and sang,

> Wink digs here and Wink digs there,
> Wink digs almost everywhere—

And so as years rolled by and tribes of men came, they discovered a bird in the woods scratching here and there and rustling dry leaves and brittle twigs. The Jungies told the tribes of men this story, and that's how we know about Wink, the lazy boy whose real name is Chewink. You can still watch him digging, especially in the springtime. So what the old folk say must be true. Na ho, I have spoken.

Why Ted-oh, the Woodchuck, Climbs a Tree

As every boy knows, Ted-oh, the woodchuck, climbs a tree when the Hot Moon blisters the grass. Did you ever hear why he does this?

Well, it's a long story, but it must be true because the Jungies all say so. Who are the Jungies? Why, they are the Little Folk that live in the woods and know everything.

There was once a woodchuck named Ted-oh who had a nice house way down under the ground. It was lined with sweet grass and had a pantry filled with all sorts of spicy roots. There was also a jar of white grubs, which Ted-oh and his wife and all the little Ted-ohs dearly loved.

Ted-oh was quite a hunter, but the game he brought in was only bugs—June bugs, black beetles, and snapping beetles. Bigger things he never wanted.

Now, it happened that Ted-oh was one day hunting around a cornfield where a tribe of Jungies had its plantation. Along the edge of the field was a tobacco bed, and in the bed was a beetle's nest. Of course all the old men know tobacco is magic and makes bugs very wise.

When Ted-oh tramped through the tobacco bed, he came to the nest of the tobacco beetles and gobbled up a mouthful. He wanted to carry them to the little Ted-ohs so that they might eat them and become wise, too.

Ted-oh trotted along through the corn and through the grass until he came to his dooryard, where he put down the bugs.

The bugs huddled together and looked up at Ted-oh in a piteous way, for they didn't want to be eaten. There was a queer, squeaking sound which made Ted-oh look at them carefully. He turned down one ear and listened. He turned down one eye and looked at the sight.

One bug was speaking right out in woodchuck language.

"Spare us," said Bug. "Spare us, and we will do great things."

"What can you do?" inquired Ted-oh.

"Anything you would like," answered the bug chief, and all the other bugs nodded their heads and wiggled their mouths.

Ted-oh began to think what he would like. His house was good, his children splendid, his health good, and his wife a pretty young woman. What more could he want?

"What more can I want except to eat you?" exclaimed Ted-oh, right out loud.

"Fun," answered Bug.

"What kind of fun?" asked Ted-oh.

"Gambling," answered Bug.

"Oh, that would be awful," said Ted-oh, noticing his wife had come to the door and was listening.

"But we can make you win every time," said Bug.

"How?" inquired Ted-oh.

"We will turn ourselves into dice, and when we are thrown, we will turn to make you win and flop to make the other fellow lose."

"Ted-oh, you spare those bugs!" said Ted-oh's wife.

"All right," said Ted-oh. "I'll spare you. Now turn into dice!"

The bugs turned into platter dice, just as nice as could be, and were black on one side and white on the other.

Ted-oh took eight of the dice and threw them on the smooth ground of his dooryard. The dice rolled over all white, which meant a perfect score.

Ted-oh was delighted and tucked the dice away in a bag he hid in his pantry. He was sure he could win all the magic charms from all the other animals and make himself Grand Chief of All Animaldom.

After awhile it became noised abroad that Ted-oh had a wonderful charm and that he had hidden it from the sight of all. Not a soul could guess what it was, not even clever Non-gwat-gwa, the fox.

Fox was very curious about Ted-oh's treasure and made up his mind he would run over for a visit and have a little gambling game with Woodchuck.

Fox had some tricks of his own and knew just how to win. He made up his mind he would gamble for treasures and finally for Ted-oh's secret charm, about which so much was said.

Over to Woodchuck's clearing trotted Fox, wearing his blandest smile and waving his tail jauntily.

"Morning, Ted-oh, my friend," said Fox.

"Morning, Non-gwat-gwa, my neighbor," answered Woodchuck.

"I came for a friendly game of dice," said Fox.

"No, no," protested Woodchuck. "I never gamble, for I lose."

"Come on, let us gamble with dice," urged Fox.

"Well, I can't very well refuse," said Woodchuck. "I'll get my platter dice, which I so seldom use."

Soon he came up with the dice and with the platter in which the dice are tossed.

"Now then," said he, "I'm ready. What will we bet?"

"Let's bet a string of beads," suggested Fox.

"All right," said Ted-oh, throwing down his wife's finest string.

Fox threw down an even better string. Then each shook the platter with a tossing motion. Fox lost and Woodchuck won, at which Fox was greatly surprised.

"Let us now bet a hundred flint-tipped arrows," suggested Fox.

"All right," said Ted-oh, throwing down a hundred arrows he had borrowed from Porcupine.

Fox threw down a full quiver of even better arrows. Then each shook the dice platter, and as before, Woodchuck won.

Again and again they gambled until Woodchuck had great heaps of pelts, long strings of wampum, many bales of fine feathers, and all sorts of trinkets and charms. Fox was vexed and felt very sore. He just wanted a chance to gamble for Woodchuck's secret treasure.

When Fox had lost time after time he scratched his face and began to think. "I must win that treasure that Woodchuck hides," he mused. Then he looked up with a sudden idea giving him new hope.

There was one thing Fox had not yet gambled, and that was his cleverness. Ho ho, he would now gamble that, so he made a long speech.

"Well is it known," he began, "that I am clever, very clever. It is because I am Fox. I have a secret: it is that my cleverness comes from eating eight magic bugs that grow on the end of branches high from the ground. On a certain day of a certain month, I climb for them, and when I see them, I eat them. Ho ho, I have a fine red coat, a fine furry tail, a long, handsome nose, and very fine ears. I can run faster than a deer, and not one of my enemies can catch me. Oh, you who are dull witted, you who are only a woodchuck, ought to be clever, to have a fine red coat, a fine furry tail, and be swift."

"I'd like to have a coat like yours and be able to outrun everybody," said Ted-oh, standing upright and looking right into Fox's eyes, so serious was he.

"Very well," said Fox. "This time you shake the dice for me. If you win for me, then you shall have the secret of my prize. If you lose for me, then you shall give me your hidden secret of which I have heard so much."

Now Ted-oh knew that if he shook the dice for Fox, the bug-dice would think he was shaking them for himself and he would only win to lose. So he said, "No, you shake for yourself."

Fox was now suspicious and began to guess that

it was the dice which were the secret treasure, so reg-
ularly did Ted-oh win.

Fox said, "Well, let's trade your treasure for
mine."

Woodchuck didn't know what to do. He was
rich with goods, so what did he care for the dice anymore? Besides, Fox's treasure up in a certain tree
sounded so much better. How splendid it would be
to have a coat like Fox's and to be able to chase
enemies.

"Are you sure your treasure bugs are in a tree?"
asked Ted-oh.

"Nothing surer," answered Fox.

"Will I grow sleek like you and have a red coat
and a fine furry tail if I get your magic bugs?"

"Nothing surer."

"All right, I will trade my secret treasure, but
first tell me the name of the tree where your treasure
is."

"It is the wonderful you-find-it tree," answered
Fox.

"Well, my treasure is this bowl of magic dice,"
confessed Woodchuck. "Everytime the owner shakes
the dice, they turn over so that he wins. When the
opponent shakes them, he always loses. Take them
and show me your tree where the eight magic bugs
grow."

"That tree is in a certain place," answered Fox.

"You must climb it on a certain day, and on a certain limb will be eight bugs—always eight together. They will talk and tell you what to do to become like me. Anyone can tell you where to see the you-find-it tree. Good-bye, I must be going."

And Fox disappeared with the magic dice, and he uses them until this day.

Woodchuck began to hunt for the magic tree, but whenever he asked the animals to tell him where it was they only replied, "You find it."

So Woodchuck still hunts for the tree, and on hot summer days anyone can see Ted-oh, the woodchuck, way up in a tree looking around for the eight magic bugs. But he has never found them yet. Little does he know that he once had them, but gave them away.

How Joeagah, the Raccoon, Ate the Crabs

AS MY GRANDFATHER USED TO SAY, MY NEPHEW, IT never pays to rejoice over the downfall of an enemy, lest he arise and devour you. Of course you can't understand that, so I'll just tell you not to dance too quick when you think a raccoon's dead.

Well, Joeagah was a raccoon. Nothing much to that, only this—Joeagah was a wise raccoon, and he knew it.

Joeagah came down from his tree one morning to get a drink of nice brook water. What should he see but a crab. Nothing much to that, my nephew, only this—the crab bit Joeagah on his lower lip. Well, there is a lot to that if you get bit. Of course Joeagah didn't mind it at all—oh, no!

Joeagah sat back and looked surprised. He was a bit peeved. He didn't like to have crabs so familiar.

Now Joeagah is a playful fellow, so he crawled up to a rock and huddled beside it. He almost looked like a rock, and the crabs didn't notice him.

Pretty soon, out came a big crab to take a look at the sky to see if it was going to rain. Up he looked when down looked Joeagah. Ho ho! Joeagah bit crab all over—and there wasn't any more crab!

"Um, um!" exclaimed Joeagah. "These meddlesome fellows taste pretty good. I think I will try some more." And try he did, until the tribe of crabs lost some of its most famous warriors, that is, those famous for being fat and appetizing.

Now, my nephew, you may notice when you grow wiser, that folk who are being eaten up grow cautious. After all, who wants to be eaten? Maybe you, but not I.

So the crabs held a council and decided to appoint a spy who should watch when Jocagah came down to drink. The spy would yell like fury and then all the crabs would stay home and hoe their own back gardens.

Joeagah soon found out that the crabs were shy and that the spy yelled whenever he came down to drink. Having found out how good crabs taste, Joeagah wanted a crab everytime he drank. He made up his mind to play a trick.

He came to the brook from another direction late one night. When the sun came out in the morning, it shone down on poor Joeagah, lying with his toes turned up and his mouth open. His ears were also open, nephew, but his eyes were shut. Poor little Joeagah! How dead he looked.

Out came the crab spy. "Ho ho!" it said. "Joeagah must have eaten too many June bugs and died. This is good news to tell." He set up a war cry, yelling, "Go-weh, go-weh, I have killed Joeagah in a terrible fight! Come all you crabs and see my victim before I scalp him!"

Out crept the crabs, very cautiously. One pinched Joeagah's tail, one pinched his ears, one pinched his feet, and one pinched his nose. But not a move did Joeagah make.

"Hai, hai!" sang the crabs. "Our enemy is dead. Let us hold a joy dance and sing of our victory."

So they sang and capered until Joeagah opened one eye just a wee bit. One crab noticed this and yelled, "Beware, Joeagah is not dead!"

"He is dead!" retorted the spy crab.

"If you think he is dead, crawl down his throat and pinch his gizzard," said the crab who had noticed Joeagah's wink.

"All right, I will," said the spy, and down the throat he crawled, giving Joeagah's gizzard a mean pinch. Joeagah did not even blink this time.

"Well, he *is* dead," boasted the spy crab, coming out. "If *you* are brave, crawl down and pinch his heart."

So the other crab crawled down and pinched

Joeagah's heart. This made Joeagah very angry. He made up his mind to start a fuss.

He waited until the crabs had started another ring-around-a-war-pole dance and were shouting their silly heads off about their victory and how glad they were their enemy was dead. This was their song:

> Joeagah, glad he's dead!
> Joeagah, glad he's dead!
> Never more he'll bite us,
> Joeagah, blunderhead,
> Joeagah, blunderhead,
> Never more he'll fight us!

Joeagah did not like that song worth a wormy crab apple. While the crabs circled around him singing their song of victory, up he jumped and began to gobble them down.

Every one of them went right down Joeagah's throat—and with Joeagah's teeth through him first.

That was the end of the crabs in that brook, and this is the end of the story.

Not much of a story? Well, nephew, my old grandfather, who fought in seven wars and had one eye, thought a lot of this tale, and he could see a lot with his one eye.

The Owl's Big Eyes

OH-O-WAH WAS A BIG SNOWY OWL, AND A CURIOUS bird was he.

Oh-o-wah wanted to be like the swan and have a long neck. He wanted to be like the white heron and have a long beak. He wanted long legs. He wanted everything other birds had.

It was a good time to want things. In those days Ra-wen-io was making the animals and the birds as they wanted to be. He walked through the forest and asked each fur-coat and feather-coat how he wanted to be. Ra-wen-io was very patient.

One day he came to the bushlands where he saw Hippity Boy, the rabbit. Rabbit was sitting on a stump beside the trail waiting for Ra-wen-io to come along.

Rabbit was singing a song, "How I'd like nice long ears and long legs like the deer! How I'd like nice long hair and sharp claws like the lynx!"

Ra-wen-io, the Masterful One, heard the plaintive song of Rabbit and came like a cloud to him and took him in his hands.

"All the feather folk, all the scale folk, all the fur folk, hear!" said the Masterful One. "Turn your heads, close your eyes, for none shall see the miracle I perform."

From his perch in the tree, Oh-o-wah looked down. "I want nice long legs, I want a nice long neck, I want a nice long beak, I want the best-feathers, I want everything better than anyone else," hooted Owl.

"Be still and close your eyes," said Ra-wen-io, while he pulled at Rabbit's ears to make them long. Then he grasped Rabbit by the waist and began to pull his legs to make them long.

Just as he was fixing Rabbit as he wished to be, Owl rolled his eyes and began to blink. He turned his head and began to look.

"Oh-o-wah, oh-o-wah," hooted Owl.

Ra-wen-io looked up and saw Owl looking. This was the forbidden thing to do. He plucked Owl from the tree and shoved his head right down into his shoulders. He looked into Owl's eyes until they grew large with fright, and then he smoothed Owl all over.

"Henceforth, now and forever," said Ra-wen-io, "all owls shall have short necks. They shall have big eyes that cannot roll, and all owls shall live in the dark where they cannot see what is done on earth when the sun shines." Then he put Owl into a hollow tree.

Ra-wen-io went back to the stump where he had left Rabbit, but Rabbit had run away the best he could, for his legs were only half finished.

To this day, Rabbit hops and is called Hippety Boy. And to this day, owls live in the dark and hate all rabbits, hunting them whenever one strays into the dark of the wood.

So that is why owls have big eyes and short necks, and why rabbits hop.

This is a short story, my nephew, but it's all the old folk know about it, so I am done. Na ho.

The Woeful Tale
of Long Tail Rabbit
and Long Tail Lynx

BEAR HAD A LONG TAIL, WOODCHUCK HAD A LONG tail, and even Deer had a long tail once. So did Panther and his cousin, Lynx, but only Panther kept his. Rabbit had a long tail once, and because he didn't know who to run around with, he lost it.

Of course there is a fox in this story, too, and that is why neither Rabbit nor Lynx have long tails anymore. Now comes the story.

Once upon a hill, a long time ago, there was a deep forest full of dark mystery and wild gooseberries. In this forest lived a mighty tribe of long-tailed four-foots. Each had a house of his own, and each minded his own business pretty well—all except Little Lynx. His companions called him Jiggon Sassy because his face was so fat and had side-whiskers.

Little Lynx had a splendid coat and a beautiful tail he kept streaming out behind or waved in the air.

He was so proud of that tail he sometimes howled all night about it, which made the snowy owls mad as hornets.

To tell the truth, Little Lynx did not have many friends, but Rabbit Boy did because he was so comical and danced around in a circle.

Never once did Rabbit Boy brag about his tail, although it was long and silken, white and fluffy, and when he jumped, it waved like a long line of gray squirrels playing leapfrog.

Now, almost anybody would think Fox would have been mean to Rabbit, but he wasn't in those days. Oh, no, he liked Rabbit Boy, and I'll tell you why.

Once a little fox got lost in the snow and Rabbit Boy found him shivering in a brush pile. What did Rabbit Boy do but coil his tail around the little fox, just like a spiral blanket. It kept him warm all night long.

When morning came, old Mother Fox came looking around for her petkin and found him as snug as could be. She thanked Rabbit Boy and said she'd tell Old Man Fox all about it.

Well, she didn't forget. Soon it was noised about all through the forest that Rabbit Boy had done another good turn.

Everybody was glad except Little Lynx. He was mad because he wanted the foxes for friends. He,

too, had seen the little fox but never thought of help-
ing him—so he was mad at Rabbit Boy for doing
what he never thought of doing. Ho ho, that's the
way with some folk.

So Little Lynx decided to get even. He made up
his mind to pick a quarrel with Rabbit Boy and get
him to fight. Then he would scratch him all to pieces
and bite off his tail.

But how should Little Lynx pick the fight? Ah,
he would make Rabbit Boy guess what he was thinking about, and if he couldn't, he would have to fight
him.

How in the world could Rabbit Boy guess? Why,
he couldn't. At least Little Lynx thought so.

Rabbit Boy was sunning his tail on a log. He
had just given it a shampoo with ashes and oil, soaked
it in spring water, and dried it in white clay.

Along came Little Lynx. Now for the quarrel!

"Humph!" sneered Little Lynx. "You think you
have the best tail in the world, don't you?"

"Good morning, Little Lynx," greeted Rabbit
Boy. "What is that you said about my tail?"

"I said you are too stuck-up over your tail. Think
it's the best in the world, don't you?"

"Oh, no, indeed I don't! Most anybody has a
better tail than mine. You, for instance, Little Lynx,
have a much nicer tail. I'd just love to have your tail,
it swishes so."

Little Lynx didn't know what to say now. He had expected to have Rabbit Boy boast, but he hadn't.

Little Lynx tried a new way.

"Think you are awfully smart, eh?" he snapped.

"Well, of course, I do know a few things," admitted Rabbit Boy.

"Humph, think you know a lot, don't you? What do you know, anyway?"

"Well," said Rabbit Boy slowly, taking in the situation with a couple of ear wiggles, "I know that Little Lynx has a beautiful tail."

"What else do you know?"

"Guess," answered Rabbit Boy, hoping to avoid further argument.

"Guess?" echoed Little Lynx. "I am going to have *you* guess a few things. And if you don't get your answers right, there will be trouble right here. Understand?"

"Yes, I guess I understand."

"You do, eh? Well guess what *Nahote* means."

"Nahote means—well, it means—why-a, it means. . . ." For a moment Rabbit Boy couldn't guess what it did mean because it was a word in the Jungie language.

"I knew you were an empty chestnut burr," sneered Little Lynx. "Hurry and guess or I'll bite you on your neck and do it hard!"

"Why bite me, Little Lynx?" asked Rabbit Boy, remembering the word now. "Nahote means 'What is it?' It's a Jungie word."

"Well, you got that right. But you can't guess what I have in my hands."

Rabbit Boy gave one look and saw a tail wriggling, so he said, "Little Lynx has a jumping mouse in his hands."

"Augh," snarled Little Lynx, squeezing the mouse to death. "You got that right, but you can't guess what bird I had for breakfast."

Rabbit Boy gave one look at Little Lynx's cheeks and saw a feather, so he said, "Little Lynx ate the sick owl that was hiding behind the gooseberry bush this morning."

"Augh," snarled Little Lynx. "You got that right, but you can't tell what flower I picked this morning."

Rabbit Boy wriggled his nose twice, sniffed a bit, and said, "Little Lynx picked the skunk cabbage down by the spring."

"Augh," sneered Little Lynx. "You got that right, but you can't tell where I slept last night."

Rabbit Boy had to look hard this time, but finally he spied some fluffy down in Little Lynx's ear. He said, "Little Lynx slept in a bed of cattails down by the swamp."

"Augh," spat out Little Lynx. "You think you

are very smart. Just the same, you don't know a thing. You don't know what I want to do right now."

"Oh, yes, I do, but my tail is dry now and I think I'll take a walk. Want to come?" inquired Rabbit Boy.

"Yes, you lead the way," answered Little Lynx. Of course he had a reason for lagging behind. He wanted a chance to pounce on Rabbit Boy's tail and nip it off.

After awhile, Rabbit Boy gave a great leap and away he went over a deep hole. Little Lynx leaped, too, but he was after the tail and didn't see the hole. He fell down into the hole—bump!

He was as mad as a lynx can ever be, for Rabbit Boy had made a wonderful leap and waved his tail so gracefully. But Little Lynx was now in a hole and needed help.

He yelled out with a mad sound in his voice, "Help, dear Rabbit Boy! Help! Your friend is in a deep hole. Oh, woe, oh, woe!"

It was right here that Old Man Fox happened along. When he heard Little Lynx wail, he wanted to laugh, but instead he sneaked right up behind a big round rock on the far side of the hole and listened.

"I'm coming," shouted Rabbit Boy.

"Let down your tail and draw me up, my dear friend," sniveled Little Lynx, with tears in his eyes and murder in his heart.

Rabbit Boy let down his beautiful tail. It was just long enough for Little Lynx to grasp it.

"Don't pull," shouted Little Lynx. "I will climb up on your tail, hand over hand."

He climbed up hand over hand and, just as he reached the top of the hole, he gave the tail a mean bite and nipped it right off.

Rabbit Boy winced because it hurt him. He staggered back ever so slightly, and as he did, Little Lynx fell down in the hole again—bump!

Old Man Fox saw the whole thing and made up his mind that his turn had come to do something.

While Rabbit Boy was scampering about and weeping over his lost tail, Old Fox called down.

"Hi," he said, "want to get out?"

"True guess," answered Little Lynx. "I'm in a terrible hole. Let down your tail and draw me out."

"Not if any fox has brains," answered Old Fox. "I saw that mean trick you played on Rabbit Boy. You are a sneaking traitor."

"Oh, help me," wailed Little Lynx. "I didn't mean it."

"Oh, no, you didn't mean it!" answered Old Fox. "But I'll help you just the same."

"Oh, please do," wept Little Lynx.

"I'll let down a grapevine," said Old Fox. "You can climb up on that."

He fixed a vine and let it down in the hole. Little Lynx was happy and climbed up. But just as he got to the top, Old Fox let go of the vine and down dropped Little Lynx—bump!

Again and again Fox teased Lynx until the poor victim was all tired out. After awhile, Old Fox said, "What will you give me if I let you out?"

"Anything," answered Little Lynx, gasping.

"All right, I'll get you out, and you go far away from the woods on the hill and never more associate with decent people. You are a liar, a thief, and a quarrelsome nuisance. What's more, you are so mean that all the meanness in the world isn't half as mean as you are, fat face, owl-fighter, tail-biter, sneak, whiney voice, fool-in-a-hole."

"Oh, get me out," whined Little Lynx.

"All right, I will, and this time you have got to jump for the grapevine and climb all the way up. If you don't get up, I will go away and let you die right where you are."

"Oh, don't let me die in a hole," wailed Little Lynx.

Old Fox let down the grapevine in such a manner Little Lynx had to make a great spring to catch hold of the end of it. Little Lynx crouched on the far side of the hole and gave a mighty leap. As he did, Old Fox rolled down the big round stone and it hit Little Lynx's tail—bump!

Little Lynx flew to the vine, feeling a terrible pain. He madly clawed his way to the top of the hole. He could go no farther, so tired was he. Besides, he had a terrible pain. He thought he'd go to sleep right there, but as he tried to coil his lovely tail about him he felt only the movement of an absurd little stump.

He arched his back and looked in a startled way down the hole. There, under the big rock, was his precious tail, broken right off and wriggling as if it were alive.

Little Lynx now gave a great cry of despair and slunk away into the tall timbers. Long did he mourn. He can be heard to this day whining and weeping in a terrible fashion.

As for Rabbit Boy, of course he felt very bad about his misfortune. But when he saw how much better it was to have a bobbed tail, he was glad enough to hug Little Lynx—but he never could find him.

So Rabbit Boy capers about, as happy as can be, and nobody calls him bobbed tail, because he jumps around so gaily. But everybody calls Little Lynx by another name now, and most people call him Bobcat.

So that is how those two lost their tails, and that is why one is glad and one is sad.

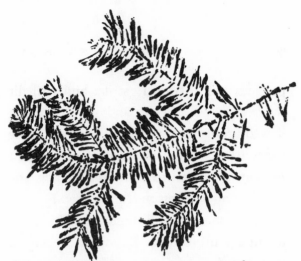

How the Rabbit's Lip was Split

NON-GWAT-GWA, THE FOX, KNEW WHERE ALL THE world's mysteries were hidden, for Fox was clever.

When Ra-wen-io, the Masterful One, was roaming the earth making it beautiful, Fox came to the house of the Tear-up-everything Monster and made a bargain with him.

"I want to make mischief today," said Fox.

"Well, here are two bags of flint," said Tear-up-everything Monster, whose Indian name was Ta-wis-ka-roo.

"What will you take for them?" inquired Fox.

"Nothing at all," answered Ta-wis-ka-roo. "You have only to roam around with the flint and make trouble. That satisfies me."

"What is flint made of?" asked Fox, wanting to know everything.

"Flint is made of the blood of my eyes," answered Ta-wis-ka-roo. "You see I had a fight with

Ra-wen-io and tried to strike him with deer horns.
But they flew at my face and hit me in the eyes. Blood
flowed and turned to flint. I was as mad as can be,
I'll tell you. To get revenge, I am going to kill all
Ra-wen-io's creatures with flint."

"That just suits me," answered Fox with glee. "I
certainly enjoy killing things myself. Tell me how to
use flint."

Ta-wis-ka-roo went into a long explanation
which fully satisfied Fox. He was now ready for a
wicked time, and after capering around in a dance to
show his thanks, he departed with the two bags.
Ho ho!

Down the trail through the underbrush went
Fox, singing like a good fellow. He swished from side
to side and he hopped up and down. It was easy to
see that he was eager to try his treasure.

After a time Fox came to the land of the Hippety tribe where Rabbit Chief lived. Rabbit Chief was the sublime ruler of all the Hippety-Hoppers, and he was a very curious fellow too, a fact which Fox well understood.

Leaping here and there through the bushes, Fox took up his station on a mossy knoll made by a fallen tree. Here he began to sing. He lifted up his face and shouted:

Nobody's around, a secret I've found!
I'm safe on this mound and so I'll expound.

Oh, fire have I, and though it's stone dry,
Should anyone try, they'd make fire fly!

Oh, fatal the dart, should man learn the art
Of bringing to mart the poor rabbit's heart.

Oh, cutter of bone, oh, cutter of stone,
To me all alone the secret is known.

Now Rabbit was munching grass not far away and his ears were lifted high to catch every word of that song, for it mentioned rabbits.

Rabbit began to wonder what Fox was doing there on that mossy mound, singing away the secrets of his inner mind.

"Ah ha!" thought Rabbit, "Fox cannot fool me with his singing. I'll sneak around behind him and

pretend I've not heard a word. Then I'll bargain for
that secret."

Cautiously hopping through the tall grass, Rabbit sneaked up behind Fox, who knew all the time
just what was going on. Soon Rabbit gave a great
leap, just as if he had come into the clearing in front
of Fox from a great distance. He pretended to be out
of breath.

"Greetings, Cousin Fox!" exclaimed Rabbit.

"Oh, how you scared me!" whimpered Fox, turning around quickly and quivering all over. "Pardon
me, I am so frightened, Cousin Rabbit."

Fox now began to fumble with his treasure and
try to tuck it under the moss.

"What are you hiding?" asked Rabbit. "Ah ha!
I know you are tucking something under the moss
there. Out with it, Cousin, or I'll have to ask you to
leave here at once. I'm Chief here, remember."

"Oh, don't drive me away," whimpered Fox. "I
only have a secret."

"What is that secret?" demanded Rabbit, wink-
ing to himself, for he remembered the words of the
song.

"It's a secret that no Rabbit should know," answered Fox.

"Why shouldn't I know your secret?" asked Rabbit, jumping toward Fox in a terrifying way and
scowling dreadfully.

"Oh, you should never know it," sniveled Fox. "You never should know, for unless you knew all about the secret it might do you terrible harm."

"Well, I guess I can manage it," said Rabbit with a swagger. "I'm nobody's fool."

"But if I let you touch my treasure and you do not know *all* about it, you might get hurt," pleaded Fox.

"Well, I'll take the chance. Out with your secret and tell me all about it."

So what should Fox do but sing his song again. Then he dug up the two bags of flint and held them forth.

"Behold the blood of Ta-wis-ka-roo!" exclaimed Fox. "Fire is in it, knives are in it, darts are in it, and unspeakable woe."

"Show me how to use it," ordered Rabbit.

Fox opened the bag and took out two pieces of gray stone.

"That's all there is to it," said Fox.

"Oh, how about that fire that's in it?" asked Rabbit.

Fox struck the flints together, and out flew a shower of sparks. Rabbit looked at the wonder with wide-open eyes. He hopped just a bit.

"Oh, how about the knives in it?" asked Rabbit.

Fox struck the flints together again, and off flew a sharp chip, shaped like a knife blade. Rabbit picked

it up and cut his foot. He hopped a lot after that,
and sucked his paw.

"Oh, oh," said Fox, "you shouldn't have done
that. I'll put my treasure away."

"No, you won't," said Rabbit firmly and with a
stern look in his eyes. "You're going to show me the
fatal darts now."

"Oh, I must put my treasure away," moaned
Fox. "If ever it cuts you, spilling blood, it means that
whoever controls flint will be able to skin rabbits as
easily as rabbits peel the bark from trees."

"I want to see those darts," demanded Rabbit in
answer, moving his ears back and frowning fiercely.

"Well, if you demand it, I'll have to show you,"
said Fox, weakening.

Fox took the flints once again and struck them
rapidly, breaking off chips. Finally a large one flew
off in the shape of an arrowhead.

"How does that work?" inquired Rabbit.

Fox put a flint chip in the end of a reed, fastened
some feathers on the other end, and tossed it at Rabbit. Rabbit stood up to catch it, but it hit the Hippety

chief right across the breast, tearing off a patch of brown fur. For the first time, Rabbit found what an arrow does.

"Ug-yaw!" squealed Rabbit, rubbing the blood from his chest. "Your secret is powerful. What will you take for it?"

"Oh, I couldn't sell it to you, Cousin," said Fox. "I don't want to part with it at all, for really, rabbits should not have it."

"But I want it," insisted Rabbit.

"Well, that being the case, you can have one of my treasure bags," answered Fox. "I'd rather not part with it, though."

"I'll take it," said Rabbit. "I guess I know a thing or two."

"Rabbit Cousin," said Fox, "you'd better look out."

"I am as wise as you, Cousin Fox," retorted Rabbit, striking the flint on a rock and getting sparks, knocking it and getting a knife, then chipping it and getting an arrowhead.

"Look out!" exclaimed Fox. "I haven't sung all my song yet."

"Keep your ancient song," replied Rabbit, starting to break off a willow rod. "I can make an arrow as well as you. See how nicely I feather it!"

Sure enough, Rabbit made a fine arrow. Fox looked on with mock anxiety.

"Oh, don't do that," he exclaimed.

"Envious, are you?" snapped back Rabbit, tossing the arrow into the air.

"No," answered Fox. "It is my great love for
you which makes me want to caution you. Listen to
the last verse of my song."

Oh, rabbits will die should rabbits ere try
Ta-wis-ka-roo's eye to feather and fly!

"Who's Ta-wis-ka-roo?" inquired Rabbit, looking up in a startled way. "You don't mean the devil,
do you?"

"Same fellow," replied Fox. "Now you're done
for! Oh, oh!"

"What will I do now?" inquired Rabbit, getting
frightened.

"You'd better burn that flint," suggested Fox.
"If you don't, it might grow so big you can't hide it.
Then hunters might find it and make darts to kill you
and maybe all the other cousins. If they get killed be-
cause of your foolishness, then they will all hunt you.
Oh, you'll have enemies enough now!"

"What did you give it to me for?" wailed Rabbit.

"You made me," said Fox. "You'd better burn
it now. You can't blame me then."

"Stay and help me," wailed Rabbit.

"No," said Fox, "I've got to be going."

Rabbit was left alone with the terrible flint. He was mighty glad Fox had suggested burning it. He built a roaring fire and threw the chunk of flint right in the middle. He waited to see if it would burn. He waited in vain until all the wood had burned down to glowing embers.

Rabbit watched to see what would happen. "I wish I hadn't asked for that flint," thought Rabbit. "It has more deviltry in it than I imagined."

Just as he said that, "Ping, pop, whee!" went the flint, exploding and scattering in all directions.

Rabbit flew to his hole with frightened leaps and, scampering down, hid in the darkness of the under-earth. He listened with quivering ears for sounds of any further tumult outside, but hearing none, began to grow more courageous.

"Ho," he thought, "flint is all burned up. I'll walk out and see the ashes of flint and make sure that Fox's prediction does not come true."

Out came Rabbit and edged up to the fire. Nothing happened. Nearer he crept, and there in the midst of the embers was the flint all cracked to a small chunk, but this glowed in an evil way.

Rabbit watched it for a moment, and then noticed that the clouds overhead had gathered for rain. Down came a drop. Down came another and hit the glowing flint with a hissing spatter.

"Snap, whee!" went the flint, cracking off a

sharp splinter. It flew straight at Rabbit's face.

"Skush" went the flint splinter, striking Rabbit right in the middle of his lip, cutting it open.

Away went Rabbit, scampering and leaping like the most frightened hippety in his whole tribe. Away he leaped and so fast did he go that for all I know he is scampering yet.

And so it happened that Rabbit got his split lip which quivers even now, and again it happened that the flint grew and scattered all over the world for Indians to use for their arrow tips.

Oh, the blood of Ta-wis-ka-roo's eye seeks out much mischief, and because of it there is a heap of woe on this green world beneath the blue sky. At least this is what the old folk say. Na ho!

Oseedah, the Rabbit Gambler

THERE IS SOMETHING ABOUT OSEEDAH THAT MAKES one wonder where his courage went, nephew. Wah! he has no courage at all, yet, my nephew, he has long ears and a short tail. Ho ho! It may be that you young people call him Rabbit, but wise old folk like me call him Oseedah.

Oseedah galloped all around every day. How he galloped! One day when he was galloping he came across two beautiful women who were dipping water from the spring. Oseedah looked at them and they looked at him. Then he began to gallop and dance and gallop and dance and wiggle his nose and wiggle his ears.

"Hee, hee, hee," laughed one of the girls.

"Tee, hee, hee," laughed the other, for Oseedah was so funny.

"Greetings and strength be to you," called both young women at once.

"Greetings and joy be to you," said Oseedah. "I am looking for a wife."

"Take me," said one.

"Take me," said the other.

Then they both fell to quarreling until Oseedah began to get fainthearted and started to run away.

"Oh, see," said one. "Lover is disgusted and is going away. Let us both take him. It is the custom for a rich man to have two wives."

So Oseedah took both young women, and they were married. He began his hunting and brought back plenty to eat and plenty to wear. The more he brought home the better his wives loved him.

They were glad he had saved a large store of goods and treasure, because he galloped so far he was in danger of being lost down a fox's throat some day. They could then have the goods and the treasure.

Oseedah, however, kept away from the foxes. He knew better than to get within reach of their sharp teeth. No, no.

Now it so happened, my nephew, that Oseedah in his travels came to a place where dwelt Sayno, whose common name you know as Skunk. Skunk was a slow fellow and did not appear very bright and so Oseedah thought him a safe friend to make.

They had a little chat and then a little stroll and then sat down together to eat. Skunk ate mice and Oseedah only ate salad. When Oseedah saw that

there would be no quarreling over food, he invited
Sayno home with him.

"Come home with me," he said. "I have plenty
of live mice in my house and I have two fine wives to
prepare them for you."

So Sayno went to Oseedah's house and sat down
to eat. He looked over Oseedah's store of treasure
and then looked over Oseedah's wives. His eyes
rolled, and after he finished his dinner he began to
entertain the young women with tales of his bravery.

"I travel far," he said, "and many a fight do I
have. I have often met Fox in my dooryard, but I
scare away Fox by just looking at him. As for that
conceited fellow, Dog, why, he runs away weeping
when I shake my head at him.   I can whip Moose
without half trying. As for the treasures I have, why, I
have more than I can tell about in a week. Of course
I am a bachelor and never talk with young ladies
unless they are interesting. Ho ho!"

Sayno was so entertaining that Oseedah's wives
both fell in love with him, but Oseedah didn't know
it. When Sayno left that night, he bade Oseedah
good-bye very tenderly. "Come over to my house and
see me," he said.

As soon as he could, Oseedah went over to
Sayno's house. After a fine supper, Sayno said,
"Come, let us gamble a bit with deer-bone dice. Let
us see who will win."

So they gambled far into the night, and Oseedah won more treasure than he ever had before. After awhile, he left Sayno's house with a promise to return.

His wives were delighted with the treasures Oseedah brought home. They decked themselves out in strings of beads and beautiful feathers, for Oseedah had won many fine plumes.

"Go again, brave Oseedah," they said. "Win and win and win, and how we will love you!"

So Oseedah went back and won again and came home with treasure. Again he went and was lucky.

"Oh, oh," said his wives, "you are just the nicest man!"

Again Oseedah went to his friend's house and gambled. But this time the more he gambled, the more he lost. Desperately he gambled and tried all the tricks known to him. He wriggled his nose and wriggled his ears and did a couple of handsprings, but without avail.

All his former winnings were lost, all he owned and much more. Finally when all was gone, Sayno proposed that they gamble for the privilege of eating one another when they felt like it. Oseedah agreed, and when the dice were thrown he lost again.

"Now, isn't that too bad?" exclaimed Sayno. "I can eat you any time I find you and am hungry. Oh, dear, that is simply awful!"

Oseedah felt very sad and bade Sayno good night.

He did not go directly home, however, for he was too ashamed. He huddled in a pile of dead branches and went to sleep.

Sayno took a stroll, for he loved the night air. His feet naturally took him to Oseedah's home.

He peered down the tunnel, which was Oseedah's front hall, and called out, "It is a fine night. Ho ho, I have gambled all night with Oseedah. I have won all his treasure. Poor fellow, if his wives ever need protection or riches, they will find shelter, food, and riches at my quarters. My house is so full of treasure the backyard is piled high."

So saying, Sayno stalked away, as skunks do, very slowly and with defiance in every step.

"What is this news?" exclaimed the wives, awakening and looking at each other. "Is Oseedah poor? Has he lost all? Has he gambled? Oh, wicked man, to gamble and lose. Oh, stupid man, not to have won!"

They went to sleep again, and in the morning decided to leave that poor place and seek a better man. They set out a breakfast of bitter herbs and burrs for Oseedah and then left home forever.

"Live with a gambler? Well, we guess not!" they both said.

Out into the beautiful morning they strolled,
meeting their friends and gossiping by the wayside.
Those friends counted for much with them. As Oseedah's wives, they were the envy of the whole woods
because Oseedah came from an old family. And his
reputed riches added to his fame.

After awhile their feet just naturally took them
to Sayno's underground castle. Outside they stood
for awhile, eyeing one another. Then they both began
to cry, feeling very sorry for themselves.

"Oh, how we need protection," they wailed.
"We have been tricked by a very wicked husband
and abused until we can hardly stand it. Boo hoo,
boo-oo hoo!"

Out came Sayno with tears in his eyes. "You
poor dear young ladies," he sniffled, with a choking
voice. "You just step in and tell me all about it."

And so the weeping wives entered Sayno's house
and sat down. They told how all their goods were
gone and how Oseedah had gambled away his fortune, leaving them destitute.

"Yes," answered Sayno, "I thought I had better
tell you last night so you could leave that loafer. Of
course, I have won all those things to which you
were accustomed. They are all here safe and sound
for you just the same. You stay here and enjoy your-
selves. You can't imagine how I despise Oseedah for
being a gambler. It's a terrible sin to lose."

"Ah, yes," said the wives, "he had no right to lose."

"If I catch him, I will bite his head off," snapped Sayno. "He gave me the privilege of eating all rabbits whenever I found them."

At this, the wives looked at one another and wriggled their noses.

"Serves them right," they said, forgetting that they were Oseedah's wives.

That night Sayno got hungry. He grabbed one of the wives—the most tender—and said, "You wicked woman, to leave your good husband!"

So poor, tender, little Oseedah woman went down Sayno's throat, and her feet and ears were added to Sayno's treasure chest. The other woman just trembled and shook and quivered with fright.

"I'd eat you, too," said Sayno, "but you are too tough. Be gone!"

So Oseedah woman went out and sought the comfort of friends, but not one would speak to her. She had sought the sympathy of a skunk and forever after was shunned.

Oseedah never gambled again. He just grew rich and got another wife who could wriggle her ears and twist her nose just like he did.

That's all my grandfather told me, and he fought in seven wars and had one eye, but he saw a lot with that. Story done.

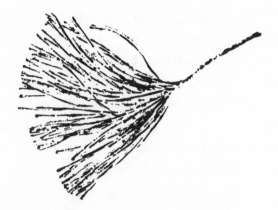

How Chief Bear Lost His Tail

So now then, my nephew, there is yet another tale left in the world, and—Ra-wen-io be thanked— it is about Nya-gwaih, the bear. You afraid of bears? Ho ho, then you'd better listen.

Once upon a hill there was a Flying Head. That's what wise old folk like me call the mischievous wind.

Flying Head was looking around, when what should he see but old Chief Bear playing with Hunter Fox. How they did play and wrestle there on the grass! Although Bear was the heavier, it was easy to see he was a duller wit. Fox ran all around him in that wrestling match.

After awhile, Bear stood on his haunches with his nose stuck in the wind. He smelled honey, and what was wrestling with a fox to eating honey? So Bear strolled up the hill and found the honey tree.

Flying Head was sitting on a rock with his hair streaming out. He said "Wheo-who-eeeeee-oooo-wee" which meant "Good morning."

Bear looked up and said, "You here?"

"Yes," answered Flying Head. "I blew a little so you would smell honey and come up here. I want to tell you something."

"Well, go ahead. I'd like to hear it."

"It's this. You ought to be careful about playing with Fox. He's a sly fellow and the first thing you know, you will be sorry you ever knew him. You know I see a lot of things."

"Oh Fox is a fine fellow," answered Bear. "We get along first rate. He doesn't eat what I do and so we never quarrel."

"Well, if you ever do find things you both like to eat, you had better look out. You'll be the sorriest man alive!"

Bear shrugged his shoulders.

"Some day I am going to blow and blow and blow," said Flying Head, "and when I whistle in your ear, you'll know Fox is going to fool you and you'll be as sorry as can be."

Bear didn't think Flying Head knew anything then. Who would think a being with a big head and long hair, no body at all, and two little feet to stand on, could have any brains? Not Bear. He would not believe in Flying Head's advice—then. But wait, and

I'll tell you how he came to change his mind. Listening, nephew?

Bear found his honey and then went down the hill where Fox was eating a fat quail.

" 'Lo," said Bear. "I guess I'll go to sleep."

"No," said Fox, "let us take a stroll."

Off they went for a long walk in the autumn woods, running and scampering and stirring up the crisp leaves. They were not hungry and didn't care how much noise they made.

After awhile they became a bit tired and sat down by a small lake to talk.

"It's a good thing we don't eat the same things," said Bear. "If we did, we might not be friendly."

"Oh, we will always be friends," said Fox. "Why should we fall out?"

"No reason," said Bear.

"Well, let us talk about what we have eaten," said Fox. "I am getting tired of wood chickens. Perhaps we can think of something else. Think of a few things, friend Bear."

"Would you like toadstools?" asked Bear.

"Awful things," said Fox.

"Would you like pond lily roots?"

"Awful things."

"Would you like blackberries?"

"Awful things."

"Would you like string beans?"

"Awful things."

"Would you like fresh fish?"

"Don't know about that—might try," answered Fox. Then he added, "Let me guess what you'd like to eat."

"Go ahead," said Bear, glad of a chance not to think.

"Would you like crawfish?" asked Fox.

"Don't like 'em."

"Would you like woodchucks?"

"Don't like 'em."

"Would you like muskrats?"

"Don't like 'em."

"Would you like wood ducks?"

"Don't like 'em."

"Would you like fresh fish?"

"Hmm, don't know about that. Never tried 'em."

"Come on, let's try to catch some now," suggested Fox.

"Well, you fish then, friend Fox."

"No, you fish, friend Bear," said Fox. "You are so much more clever than I am. Besides, your tail is long enough for a fishline, while mine is just a clumsy club."

Now if there was one thing above another in this world of crab apple trees and goose feathers that Bear was proud of, it was that beautiful tail of his. Why, it was long enough to lasso an elk or tie the door shut. But generally, to keep it out of burrs and out of the claws of wildcat kittens, Bear kept it coiled up.

Being flattered, Bear consented to have his tail used as a fishline. Fox tied a hook on the end of it and pointed out a stump in the lake where Bear could sit and fish.

Bear swam out to the stump and let down his tail. Fox remained ashore with a basket in which to pack the fish. Yes, he *said* so, but in reality Fox meant to eat the fish as fast as they were flopped ashore. O nephew, the fox never fools himself!

How fast those fish did come! There were all sorts—mullet, catfish, sturgeon, minnows, trout, white fish, black fish, blue fish, yellow fish, and green fish; flat fish, broad fish, long fish, tall fish, and another kind of fish I don't know, so it doesn't count.

After awhile, the fish stopped biting and the wind started to blow. Flying Head was getting busy.

Oh, how that wind blew and how it whistled and how the water splashed on Chief Bear's coat!

In a little while the wind stopped blowing and the lake grew calmer and calmer and calmer until its surface was like a piece of glass. All the time it was getting colder and colder, and then the wind came up again. But not a ripple did it make on the surface of the lake—not a tiny ripple. Maybe you can guess why.

Bear was growing uneasy because he had stood on one foot so long. He shifted his foot, and as he did, he felt a big bite. He jerked on his tail to flop the fish ashore, but no fish came.

"Ho ho," he thought, "it must be a big fish." So he gave another jerk on the line. Nothing came. He pulled harder, but still his tail was held fast.

"It must be a monster," he thought. "Well, I'm glad I didn't eat those little fish. This one will be mine."

With a sort of cold hope in his heart, Bear gave a big lunge forward, but this only caused a terrible strain on his tail. Bear was cross now, and crosser, too, because he was as hungry as a bear. That fish wouldn't come out.

Again Bear strained and pulled and lunged and then gave a leap from the stump. He felt a terrible pain, just as if he had come to the parting of the ways. There was a snap, a rip, a tear, a sting—and away tumbled Bear, right on top of the water! Over and over he rolled, all the time saying disgraceful things about this world of crab apples and goose feathers. Ho ho!

Bear stood up and his feet got as cold as ice. There was no water. He was standing on ice. He went to the place where he had been fishing, and there he saw something sticking in the ice. It was his tail! Oh, oh! By all the blessed mullets, what Bear did say!

Bear was so angry now he forgot it was cold. He only had one desire and that was to find Fox and chew off his left ear. If he could do that, he would make Fox sit in the water and freeze off his fluffy red brush, *that's* what *he'd* do.

But the meek little fox had innocently eaten all the little swimmers and left nothing but their prickly bones. He thought he would leave the country and let Bear have the big fish.

Bear now felt he had lost a tail and a friend, and he was sore. He rubbed his face with his paw.

Flying Head came by and sat in a tree. He looked at Bear, and Bear looked at him.

"Told you so, told you so," blew Flying Head. "What did I say about trying to eat what Fox did?"

"Never had a chance," answered Bear.

"That's the answer," said Flying Head. "Never had a chance!"

"Well, I'm hungry and sleepy," said Bear, "and I am mad."

"Go to bed and suck your paw," said Flying Head.

So Bear went to sleep in the cave of the bear tribe. When he awoke next spring, he saw that all the little bears born that winter had no tails. Bear wasn't so grieved, but he and his kin have remained tailless. And they have been cross as bears, too.

That's all, nephew.

The Buffalo and
the Mean Old Bear

ONE FINE MORNING IN THE EARLY AUTUMN OLD
Chief Bear felt so cross that he wanted to fight with
someone. Oh, he was so cross that he didn't like anything in the whole green world!

Chief Bear made up his mind to tell everybody
just what he thought of them, and to do it in such an
ugly manner that nobody would mistake his meaning.
Why should he, a chief, mince matters?

There was no reason at all, so far as he could see.
But right here, nephew, let your wise old uncle observe that cross people can't see very far or very
clearly.

Well, anyway, Chief Bear was so ugly that he
thought he could fight all the wildcats in the world,
and all the panthers, and all the wolves and wolverines, and all the bad badgers, too. Oh, if he could just
set his eyes on the whole bunch of them—he'd just
chew them up!

"Grr-rrr, oof!" Bear growled.

Trotting along the river, Chief Bear looked to the east and he looked to the west. He looked to the cold way and he looked to the warm way, and by and by he saw a black speck far ahead. Ah, here was quarry. Now would come the fight! More "grr-rrr" and more "oof." Such were Chief Bear's mad noises— "Grr-rrr, oof—" just like that!

On and on he trotted toward the speck. After awhile he saw it was a stranger from the wide grass-lands—Buffalo.

Chief Bear didn't know before why he was so mad, but now he knew. Ho ho! A stranger had come to his hunting grounds, to Bear's own special game preserve! He might eat all the grubs and discover all the honey trees. More "grr-rrr" and more "oof."

After awhile, Bear saw that Buffalo was a whole lot bigger than he thought he was. Buffalo was a big fellow and had wicked horns.

This made Bear very angry, for what business had Buffalo to have sharp horns? Bears did not have them. It mattered not that bears had sharp teeth and sharp claws. Oh, no! This to Bear was all right, but to Bear it wasn't right for Buffalo to have sharp horns.

Bear grew more angry than ever and growled away to himself as he trotted toward Buffalo.

Bear came to the riverbank where the cliffs

were very high, just as they are on the great river
Jennesceo. Here he saw Buffalo feeding on the tall
grass and rolling his eyes this way and that way.

"Hi, there, you old grass-grubber!" snarled Bear.

"Good morning, Chief Bear," answered Buffalo.
"What's your grouch?"

"It's a wonder you can't be polite," snorted Bear.
"I tell you, you are a mean old mussy-neck and your
tail is full of burrs."

"Well, what's that," ruminated Buffalo, "so long
as the sky is blue and the grass is green and there is
cool water in the pleasant river?"

"It's a lot to me," answered Bear. "You are in
my hunting preserve. Get out!"

"You want this grass?" inquired Buffalo.

"No, you old wool-head," snapped Bear. "You
know as well as I grass isn't fit for warriors to eat."

"Oh, so?" answered Buffalo, as he munched. He
thought to himself as he chewed away, "My, old
Bear is cross today!"

"I am not cross," retorted Bear, reading Buffalo's thoughts.

"I didn't say a word," replied Buffalo.

"Yes, but you thought a lot," said Bear.

"Well, what I think is my own opinion and I
only think what you make me think."

"You will call me names, you old flail-tail. Take
that!" And Bear gave a vicious swing with his paw.

Buffalo looked up and thought, "My, Bear is in a mean mood today! I've half a notion to kick him in the ribs."

"So you want to kick me in the ribs, eh?" snarled Bear, reading Buffalo's thoughts. "Just for that, I'll fight you, you impudent old mud-wallower!"

"I don't want to fight," said Buffalo. "I only want grass, water, and pleasant weather."

"Ho, you shaggy-topped coward!" laughed Bear. "I can see you are afraid of me. I think I'll eat you for supper and throw what's left to the wolves—if they'll eat such wormy meat."

"My," thought Buffalo, "Bear is getting fierce. For two bites of sassafras leaves I'd let him feel one of my sharp hoofs."

"So you still want to kick me?" growled Bear. "I never saw such a mean person as you. You are nothing but a plain skulking possum. Just for that, take this!" And Bear stuck his claws in Buffalo's nose, making it bleed.

"Now, look here!" roared Buffalo. "I am having enough of you. If you don't stop your bothering, I'll make you sorry."

"So you threaten me?" growled Bear. "Just for that, take this!" And he jumped on Buffalo's back and bit his neck.

Buffalo shook him off and lowered his head, pointing one sharp horn right at Bear's left eye.

"Look out for me now!" shouted Buffalo. "I am a very patient man, but when I get mad, something is bound to happen. It won't be anything bad for me, either!"

Buffalo thought he would hook Bear in the side and tear off a big patch of skin to give him something besides a bad temper to nurse.

"So you plan to kill me?" roared Bear, reading Buffalo's thoughts.

"I didn't say so," answered Buffalo, "but if you persist in your meanness, it is quite likely that I can't save you from an awful thumping!"

"Ho, ho, ho!" laughed Bear, with a mean tone to his voice. "So *you* are going to thump *me?*"

"Well, I am not going to stay here and let you cut my coat and cut my tail and tear holes in my collar without some revenge," answered Buffalo.

Bear now ran all around Buffalo and paused for a moment as he lifted himself upon his haunches and doubled up his fists.

Buffalo hugged the edge of the cliff as if shrinking from wicked old Bear. And it must be said that Buffalo looked worried all right, for when bears stand on their hind legs and double up their fists, somebody is going to get hurt.

Buffalo, still at the edge of the cliff, lowered his head and pointed his sharp horns right at Bear's soft belly. "I'll hook him there," thought he.

Bear read Buffalo's thoughts and dropped down on all fours. With a wild rush he sprang at Buffalo, jaws open and claws ready. The conflict was on!

"Grr-rrr, oof!" roared Bear as he leaped.

"Phmoof, waaa!" bellowed Buffalo, jumping high in the air.

Bear was filled with speed, and his spring was a master leap. He landed where Buffalo had been only an eye wink before.

But Buffalo had jumped, too, right over Bear, and when Bear got where he thought Buffalo was, Buffalo wasn't there. There was nothing but space right over the deep river gorge—and into this space Bear soared.

Far out Bear went and, having no wings, he began to fall. Down he fell, down, down, down.

Buffalo turned around and looked for his foe. He went to the brink and, rolling his eyes as buffaloes do, he saw Bear dropping like a furry ball.

Bear plunged into the deep pool below, and it was two dozen eye winks before he came up again. Bear was a bad diver, and instead of going head first, he had gone belly first, and a terrible flop it was.

When Bear came up, he had lost all his mean thoughts. They had been knocked plumb out of him. He was just a weeping old Bear who felt sorry for himself.

Out he crawled and clawed his way up a dead

pine because there was no escape except by swimming
a long way. Now he sought a roosting place in the
pine where he could catch his breath.

"Hi there, old flop-diver," called Buffalo. "Any
way I can help you?"

"Weep, weep!" was all Bear could say as the
tears rolled down his cheeks.

"Hi there, old bug-eater, old crosspatch, old
can't-fighter, old toad-eater, old sticky face," called
out Buffalo. "Come up here and fight like a man!
What do you mean by running away like a coward?"

"Weep, weep," was all Bear could say as the
tears rolled down his cheeks. Then he slid down the
tree and jumped in the river and swam far away.

After that, you can bet, Bear kept away from
Buffalo. He always said he wouldn't associate with
people who called others by such mean names as Buffalo did. Grr-rrr, oof!

The Porcupine's Quills

"Get out of my way, Gray One," growled Bear. "Hurry up, hurry up!"

"I don't like to hurry," answered Gray One, the soft-skinned porcupine.

"Then I'll step on you," said Bear. "You can't block this path."

"It's my path, I made it," said Gray One.

"Well, if I want to walk in it, I will," said Bear gruffly.

"Let me take my time then," begged Gray One.

"I'll take my own time," said Bear, stepping right on Gray One, and sticking his claws right in the poor fellow's back.

"Oh," groaned Gray One, "everybody abuses me."

And so Bear went on, laughing at soft-skinned Gray One who would not hurry. But Gray One did not laugh. He wept, for some other four-foot was coming along.

"Get out of my way, Gray One," snarled Bobcat.

"Oh, I don't like to hurry," pleaded Gray One.

"Oh, don't block the path," said Bobcat.

"It's my own path, I made it," wept Gray One.

"Well, a path's a path, and I'll walk in it if I want to," said Bobcat with a grin, as he stuck out his claws.

"Let me take my time," pleaded Gray One.

"After I pass by," said Bobcat, grabbing Gray One by the neck and flinging him aside, at the same time batting him with one sharp-clawed paw.

"Oh, oh," moaned Gray One, weeping. "Everybody abuses me."

One by one the animals stalked down Gray One's path, pushing him aside and doing him some injury.

Now Gray One was not a bothersome fellow at all. He was just soft and good natured. He disliked to hurry, for what was the use? Anyone who hurried got there sooner and only had to come back, and so life became just hurry-scurry to him.

Gray One had a coat of fine soft wool, like a possum, but he was no possum. He looked his foes right in the eye.

Gray One could climb trees, and when he wanted to do so, he could run as fast as Fox, which is very fast. Most of the time, however, he didn't want to run, he just didn't want to.

Along came Red Fox and saw Gray One licking his scratches.

"Hi, there, Gray One," said Fox. "What's the matter?"

"They all scratch and bite me," said Gray One.

"Never mind that," said Fox. "Do me a favor."

"What's that?" inquired Gray One.

"Climb that pine and pick off a cone."

"What for?"

"Just because I say so," said Fox.

"All right," answered Gray One moodily. "I'll go."

Up he went with great agility and plucked a cone.

"Thank you," said Fox. "You are a pretty fine fellow. Say, would you like to be my friend?"

"And have you eat me?" inquired Gray One.

"No," answered Fox. "You see, I don't like Bobcat and I don't like Bear, while Dog just gets me mad. I do not choose friends very often, but I do like you."

"I wonder," replied Gray One. "Well, what next?"

"Roll over in the clay," said Fox.

"And get my woolly coat all plastered?" inquired Gray One.

"That's it exactly," said Fox. "Go on and do as I say."

"Oh, all right," said Gray One. "Just so long as you don't bite me or stick your claws through my skin."

"You'll soon forget your skin," said Fox, as he watched his friend roll over and over in the mud.

After awhile Fox began to laugh. "Ho ho," he roared. "You look like a chunk of mud rolled off a clay bluff. Well, that's just what I want, ho ho!"

Fox now began to pick thorns off a haw tree, and after he had a big pile of them, he peeled off the bark. The ends of the thorns wouldn't peel, but most of the thorn showed up nice and white.

Fox sorted the thorns and then started to stick them into Gray One's mud coating. After a time he finished the work and stepped back to admire his effort. Gray One looked like a formidable beast, ready to frighten anyone.

"Now, look here," said Fox. "Remember I'm your friend. You just do as I say, and don't you ever crawl in my bed or chase me. Now then, I am going to sit on that hummock of grass and watch the fun when Bear and Bobcat come back from hunting."

"What will I do?" asked Gray One, feeling uncomfortable in his prickly coat.

"Just as you have always done. Keep in your own path and take your time," answered Fox.

Gray One dried out and his coat fitted better. He crouched in his path and waited.

Along came Bear, grouchy as ever that food was so scarce.

"Get out of my way, Gray One," he snorted.

"I don't like to hurry," came the answer.

"Then I'll step on you," said Bear. "I told you once before that you can't block the path."

"Well, it's my path, I made it," said Gray One, crouching in the grass.

"Go ahead, Bear, toss him out," shouted Fox. "Don't take orders from the soft-skinned one!"

"You are no friend of mine," growled Bear, "but your idea is a good one." So saying, he grasped Gray One and lifted him up.

"Grr-oof, grr-oof," snorted Bear. "What is this that pierces my hands?" And he put Gray One down.

"Let me alone," screamed Gray One.

"I'll let you alone all right," said Bear, trotting off and licking his punctured paws.

"Go on and eat him alive," shouted Fox, laughing until he rolled off his grassy knoll.

"I'll eat you!" snorted Bear.

"Come on and catch me," replied Fox, laughing the louder.

Who should come along next but cross old Bobcat.

"Get out of my way, Gray One," he shouted.

"I'll stay right here," came the answer.

"Oh, you will, will you? We'll see about that."

"Go on and give him a good bite," called Fox.

"You are no friend of mine, but your idea is good," snarled Bobcat, leaping upon Gray One and giving him a savage bite.

"Rao-ow-spputt!" spat Bobcat. "What is this that pierces my mouth? Oh, those thorns have torn me terribly. Oh, my tongue!"

Bobcat fell to plucking out the thorns, but they had grown barbs, and such a sputtering was never heard before.

Fox rolled over and over with laughter until his sides ached. "Eat him up, the monster!" he shouted, and laughed again.

"I'll eat you!" snarled Bobcat. "You fooled me."

"Come on and catch me, I might make a good meal," laughed Fox.

Then who should come along but Dog, the matchless hunter.

"Get out of my way, Gray One," snapped Dog.

"I'll stay right here," came the answer.

"So you want another shaking?" asked Dog.

"Let me alone," replied Gray One.

"Go on and give him the shaking of his life," called out Fox.

"You are no friend of mine," said Dog, "but your idea is a good one."

So saying, he gave a great leap and landed right on Gray One, his jaws snapping on the animal's neck.

"Mmmmmmmmm-ee, yow yip!" yelled Dog. "What horrible thing has pierced me all over like arrows?" And he leaped away whining, to pluck out the thorns, but the thorns all had cruel barbs.

As Dog wept and whined, Fox rolled over and laughed, "Say, Dog," said he, "why don't you just eat up that soft, flabby Gray One?"

"I'll eat you!" snapped Dog, twisting into knots, so painful were the stings of the thorns.

"Come on and catch me," invited Fox, but Dog was in no mood for a chase. He had other troubles, and they were thorny ones.

Fox scampered off to seek more foes to set on Gray One. But the word had gone forth that Gray One had become Prickly One and was to be respected.

"So now," said Fox, "I have made a man of you. You just do as you please and treat all my enemies as though they were yours. You gave me the magic pine cone that gives me great speed. I gave you magic hair that will let you take your time and command your own path."

"Thanks," said Prickly One. "I always did like to take my time."

And so, my nephew, Porcupine takes his own time and anyone who argues with him will have troubles of his own, and they'll be prickly ones, too. So it is said by the wise ones. Na ho.

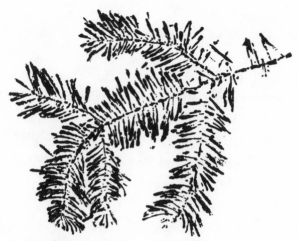

The Mink and the Eagle

MINK WAS LONG AND CLUMSY, BUT IN THOSE DAYS, as now, Mink was very fond of rabbits. He loved to nibble at good rabbit meat. Oh, yes, Mink was a savage fellow. But Rabbit in those days was so swift that Mink seldom caused the hippety tribe much trouble.

It so happened, my nephew, that Mink's little son was hungry. There had been a famine and for many weary days little Mink Boy had not eaten even a mouthful.

Father Mink felt bad about this, for he wanted Mink Boy to grow up and be a powerful hunter. So what should old Mink do but sneak out from his home in a hollow log and vow not to return until he had secured fat Rabbit. Of course rabbits always find things to eat and can grow fat.

Mink paused beneath a tall tree and listened. He smelled Rabbit somewhere. He looked in every direction, quivering all over. He did not know that in the tree just overhead was the home of Raccoon, nor did he know Raccoon's nest was lined with rabbit skins, but, strange to relate, such was the truth.

Raccoon suspected he had a caller below on his front doorstep. He crept out of his hole and looked down. Sure enough, there was clumsy old Mink, smelling for all the world like burned meat.

Ho! Raccoon made up his mind to fix Mink. He threw down a stone and hit Mink right on the top of the head. And poor Mink just rolled over and fainted away. Raccoon laughed and went back into his nest.

After awhile, Mink began to revive, and, feeling rather weak, crawled into a little hollow log. Here he went to sleep, but having a bad dream about being chased by Rabbit, he woke up with a start and smelled Rabbit once more. He came out of the log. Just as he did, he heard the whir of heavy wings and mighty Eagle swooped down.

With a movement quicker than usual, Mink slipped into the hollow log. Eagle, however, was not to be denied, and with a sudden pounce he grasped the hollow log and lifted it into the air, flying away with it.

Far through the blue flew Eagle. High he went, until in a distant land of high mountains, he landed upon a lofty peak.

Throwing down the little log, he hastened to his nest where two eaglets were crying for food. How they did scream and cry!

"Oh, Father," wept one eaglet, "bring us food."

"Oh, Father," said the other, "since Mother was killed by Bobcat, we have had no meat."

"Be still," said old Eagle. "I have something for you in that hollow branch I have thrown over there. Wait a few winks and he who is inside will try to crawl away—then I will catch him for you."

Mink listened with his sharp ears and nodded his aching head up and down, saying, "Nobody is going to eat me if I can help it!"

Old Eagle waited a long time and then flew away for more food. This was Mink's great chance for some food for himself. Young eagles would taste good, and besides, they were a rare dish. Mink smacked his lips as he sneaked out and slunk up to the nest.

He saw two young eaglets not yet able to fly. They looked lean and lonesome. Mink looked at them and then thought of Mink Boy, far away. Mink shed a tear and decided to go hungry.

Running up to the nest, he said in his most friendly voice, "Hi, there, eaglets! Are you hungry? Look at me, I am a mighty hunter and will bring you game."

The eaglets looked frightened.

Mink looked about and with his keen eye discovered some rock mice on a ledge far below. They were eating bones fallen from the nest of Eagle.

Down sneaked Mink in his slow, clumsy manner and by dint of good fortune captured three mice. These he brought back up the face of the cliff. Two he gave the eaglets, and one he ate himself. He felt much better and began to entertain the eaglets with songs and comical dances. Just as he was about to sing his funniest song there was the whistle of wings, and Mink darted for his refuge in the hollow branch.

Long did Mink stay there, wondering how he might ever get home, for he knew that it was far, far

away. Indeed, he felt very sad. He feared Mink Boy
had starved to death while he was eating mice and
feeding the children of Eagle.

After awhile he decided the best way to get
home was to crawl down the moutain and follow the
great river to its source, climb the next mountain
range, and then descend to the valley where he saw
trees that looked like home. But, alas, Mink did not
know that many weary miles of travel were between
him and his abode. Nevertheless, he started. Eagle
was away, and all was safe.

Long did Mink travel until one day, tired and
hungry, he curled up on the top of the mountain
across the valley from Eagle's peak and went to sleep.
He slept heavily.

Along came Eagle, and spying a tender morsel,
swooped down and picked up Mink. Back flew Eagle
to his nest on the peak.

"Oh, good!" cried the eaglets. "You have
brought Mink back to us. We feared he had crawled
into his branch and gone into a long sleep."

"Is this the friend who fed you?" inquired old
Eagle.

"He is our friend who fed us and danced for us,"
cried both eaglets. "Save him for us!"

"So you are the fellow who helped my boys!" exclaimed Eagle.

"Yes," answered Mink. "I have a boy of my own

who is starving. I wish I might find him, but it is so far away."

"Well," said Eagle, "I have been waiting for you to come out of your branch so I could talk to you. I knew that you had fed my eaglets. Do you want to go home?"

"I want to go," answered Mink. "I was on my way when you caught me."

"All right," said Eagle. "I will take you home, but before you go, I am going to do many things for you."

"What are you going to do?" inquired Mink, his heart beating very fast.

"I am going to make you swift, and your short legs shall be swifter than Rabbit's, swifter than Fox's, swifter than Otter's," said Eagle.

"That will be fine!" exclaimed Mink.

"Yes, and I am going to give you power to escape your enemies though they be upon you. They may see you and open their jaws to crush you, but when they wink, you will be far away," promised Eagle.

"That will be fine!" exclaimed Mink.

"And besides that, you shall no longer be clumsy," said Eagle.

So saying, Eagle fanned Mink with his wings and danced around him. Finally he said, "Here is medicine. Take it."

Mink swallowed the medicine and quivered all over as it gave him power. Such medicine Eagle alone can give.

Eagle now took Mink by the neck and flew far over the mountains to Mink's old home and dropped him down gently right by his old log.

"Now," said Eagle, "I am going to put some of my down feathers on your chest, so you won't forget me." And Eagle put white down feathers on Mink's brown chest. Then he flew back to his eaglets.

Mink looked about for his boy. He nosed into the log, but found it empty. After awhile he heard a sound, and slipping quickly under the leaves, awaited the coming of the sound maker. Nearer the sound came. Something was being dragged over the leaves.

Mink looked sharply, and very sharp were his eyes. He saw another brown mink dragging a raccoon. Mink came out of hiding and ran up to the stranger.

"Greetings, stranger," said Mink. "You appear to be going somewhere."

"Greetings, stranger," said the other. "You appear to be hungry. Sit down and eat with me."

The two began to eat the raccoon, when Mink looking up, inquired if the stranger had seen a poor starved boy in the nearby log.

"Oh, yes," said the stranger. "I lived there and was hungry. My father went away long ago but never came back. I grew up and began to hunt for myself."

"Then you are Mink Boy!" exclaimed old Mink. "How did you learn to hunt?"

"I was very hungry. But after awhile, mice began to run into my log and I fed upon them until I grew strong. After that, an old eagle dropped down a bag of medicine roots which I ate. Then I became a mighty hunter. I can run faster than Rabbit, faster than Fox, and I'm swifter than Otter. I think I can outrun you now, Father."

"We'll see about that," said old Mink, giving his boy a hug.

And so you know now, O son of my older sister, just how Mink grew wise and swift—yea, more cunning than all creatures. Na ho.

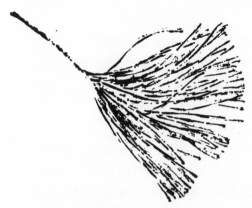

The Box Tortoise's Shell

Box Tortoise wouldn't talk to any of the fur folk or the feather folk. He was suspected of talking to newts and frogs.

Now there was a special reason why the wood folk wanted to talk to Tortoise. He had a whistle and also a secret. There were times when he had been seen in the water or on a mossy log, whistling just like a bird—only he whistled much better.

All the forest folk wanted to know about that whistle and also about the secret. They resolved to surround his pond and just make Tortoise tell all about himself.

Old Wolf was chief in that part of the country, and it fell to his lot to call the council which should force Tortoise to be more sociable.

It always happens that way, O nephew. When a man just minds his own business and goes along about it, others think he is a sly mischief maker, especially

if he has a good trick, like whistling better than anyone else. Then if it is discovered he has a secret, too,
woe betide him. The whole neighborhood will want
to know all about it, and tongues will wag until it
is told.

Well, in the woods, tongues did wag and tails did
wiggle, ears flapped, and noses twisted, all because
Tortoise minded his own business and whistled so
well.

Around the pond circled Beaver, around it circled Otter, then came Muskrat and Weasel, Mink
and Fisher, Pine Marten and Wolverine. Up on the
shore were Fox and Raccoon, Woodchuck and Gray
Squirrel, Bobcat and Bear. In the brushland nearby

was Rabbit. Above the pond flew the feather folk,
led by Osprey.

In the pond and around the log were Bullfrog
and Lizard, Salamander and Eel, Billfish and Water
Snake.

Tortoise looked out at the land and saw visitors.
He looked at the water along the shore and saw visitors. He looked about his log and saw visitors. He
looked up in the air and saw visitors. But he just
minded his own business. He wanted to whistle and
he did whistle, while the visitors looked on and chattered.

"Greetings," called out Wolf, from the shore.
"We have come to visit you. Come join our party."

Tortoise said nothing.

"Why do you always keep aloof from us?" asked
Bear.

Tortoise said nothing.

"You must be very bad to keep from talking to
us. What's the matter with you?" asked Woodchuck.

Tortoise said nothing.

"Where'd you get your whistle?" asked Raccoon,
wishing he had it.

Tortoise said nothing.

"You have a secret," asserted Otter. "We fur
folk want to know all about it. You must be a very
bad person to keep a secret from your dear cousins."

Tortoise said nothing.

"People like you ought to be punished," said Beaver. "Who will help torture Tortoise?"

"I will," yelled everybody. "I'll fix him!"

"What will you do?" inquired Wolf of each chief at the council.

"I'll chew off his legs," called out Rabbit.

"I'll slap him flat with my tail," called Beaver.

"I'll suck his blood," chirruped Weasel.

"I'll gnaw his shell," chattered Squirrel.

"I'll pick out his eyes," squawked Heron from the marsh.

"Now you hear what's going to happen!" exclaimed Wolf.

Tortoise said nothing. He just kept on whistling on his flute.

"Ready now, warriors," shouted Wolf. "Catch Tortoise for the torture!"

Away rushed the fur folk, the feather folk and the skin folk, in a wild charge upon Tortoise. Claws were ready, jaws were ready, bills were ready, and so were fangs.

The warriors assailed Tortoise, who simply put his flute in his pocket, drew in his head and his legs, and silently dropped into the pond, going down, down, down, until he sank in the mud.

The warriors swam or flew back to their posts along the shore.

"He is full of evil," whistled Woodchuck.

"We'll get him tomorrow," croaked out Crane.

"Leave it to me," said Osprey. "I'm chief around here."

So they all waited until another day had come. Out came the sun, and up came Tortoise to bask in its warmth. There he was on the log, as unconcerned as you please. When he was warmed all the way through, he did a little dance and whistled. Then he swam ashore, where he crawled under a log.

Beneath the log in a wonderful cave lived Jungie, the Chief of the underearth Little People.

"Greeting," said Jungie. "I'm glad you came."

"Greeting," said Tortoise, "I'm glad you are here."

"Anything wrong?" asked Jungie.

"Yes," answered Tortoise. "All those people out there are trying to make me tell all my business. They want my whistle and want my secret."

"I saw the whole thing," replied Jungie. "All you have to do is to say nothing."

"I think I'll ask you for some thread," said Tortoise. "There's going to be trouble, and I might need it."

"Is your secret safe?" asked Jungie.

"Yes," answered Tortoise, pulling out a little needle. It was the first splinter needle in all the world and was made of bird bone, sharpened at both ends with a hole in the middle.

"Here's your thread," said Jungie, handing over some fine sinew, well finished. "I made it myself from the backbone tendons of a deer."

"Good-bye, and thank you," said Tortoise, the silent one, tucking his secret inside his shirt.

Many were the glinting eyes that watched Tortoise crawl back to the pond and then swim to the log.

"We saw you!" called out Wolf. "We know where you hide your treasures! Under a log—there's where you hide them. Ho ho! Now we shall kill you!"

So they all called him names and made fun of him.

"Leather-neck," called out Chipmunk.

"Crawl-in-a-box," laughed Crow.

"No-ears-at-all," whistled Rabbit.

"Can't-talk-to-his-neighbors," chattered Raccoon.

"Hard-shell," called out Woodchuck.

Tortoise said nothing.

"Pounce on him now!" called Wolf, and down sped Osprey like an arrow shot by the Thunderer.

Tortoise had just time to crawl in his shell and shut the door when Osprey seized him and lifted him high into the air. Then hovering over a great rock, Osprey dropped Tortoise and saw him smash on the stony ground far below.

Tortoise was all cracked up, and his shell was a sight. He was almost like jelly inside. Still, he had his wits about him and rolled over into the water and sank. Lucky for him, too, for just then down swooped Osprey to gather him in.

Tortoise crawled along under the water until he came to a sunken log. Here he sat down and took out his needle and thread. Though he was pretty sore from his fall, nevertheless he sewed himself up. The seams you may still see on his shell, for he did a fine piece of work with his needle and thread—this wonderful secret of his that Jungie gave him.

After awhile Tortoise crawled into the sunken log and found the house of the underwater Jungies, who nursed him back to health.

"When you recover," said the good chief of the underwater Jungies, "you must go far ashore and never come near the water. Seek out a woodland Jungie and live with him in the leaves."

So Tortoise crawled ashore and has ever since lived in the woods, friendly only with Jungie people, and talking to no one at all, save them.

Fur folk, feather folk, and scaly folk are now sorry they treated him so and often try to make amends for their curiosity of old. They understand now that it is just his hard shell that makes him so.

But Tortoise says nothing to any of them.

That's all, nephew. Lots of things to think about, eh? Tortoise may have his good points, but who wants to be one? Maybe you, but not I, nephew.

How the Bluebird Gained the Color of the Sky and the Gray Wolf Gained and Lost It

IN THOSE WAY-OFF LONG-AGO DAYS WHEN YO-AN-JA, our world, was young, Ra-wen-io, the Creator, made all the birds and animals of one color, but he filled the world with all colors.

No, my nephew, the All-Wise One was not careless. He only wanted the fur folk and the feather folk and the skin folk and the shell folk and the crawly folk to find the colors they liked best of all. He made things beautiful and good, and when his little folk found what was handsome and good, he let them wish hard to be like that.

Now listen to what Jenny-er-ye did. It is good.

Long time ago, Jenny-er-ye had a gray coat of feathers. All creatures had the same kind of coat, and this caused great confusion. All kinds of squirrels and rats were mixed up, and one bird couldn't tell his mate from another bird's mate.

All the little folk grew quarrelsome and fought.

Ho ho, that's why little beasts no bigger than your two fingers fight so hard now. They got mad and stayed mad, and all their children were born cross. But they are only cross now when we, the two-leg folk, bother them.

Yes, Jenny-er-ye was gray and not as happy then as she is now. One morning in the springtime she looked up at the sky. She saw it was blue, oh, a shining, lustrous blue! Now it was her morning to sing, and this is what she sang:

> The sky is blue and good to see.
> Oh, that my coat might lovely be
> Like the sky. . .

She sang so beautifully on the branch of the old hemlock that Ra-wen-io heard her song.

"Oh, little bird," he said, "would you like to be beautiful like the sky?"

"I'd love to be beautiful like your sky, Ra-wen-io," said the bird.

"What would you give me to be like the sky?" asked the All-Wise One.

"I'd give you all my thanks and try to please you always," said Jenny-er-ye.

"Every morning for four mornings, when you dip in the lake for your bath, fly back to this branch and sing to me. Say, 'Ra-wen-io, I am glad I am going to be like the sky.'"

Jenny-er-ye looked down at the lake and for the first time saw that it was blue like the sky and that clouds seemed to float in its depths.

"Ah," she thought, "the lake is blue, and, by dipping in, my feathers will be wet with the color of the sky."

The next morning Jenny-er-ye dove bravely into the lake and wet her feathers with its spray. She flew back to the trees and preened in the sun. But as she dried, her heart was sad with disappointment. Not a sign of blue could she see. Nevertheless she sang, "Ra-wen-io, I am glad that I am going to be like the sky."

The next day, and the next day, she bathed and she sang, but not a sign of any color could she see. Her heart was filled with disturbing doubt. Yet on the fourth morning she plunged in and then flew back to the tree to dry in the morning wind. She was still wet and still gray. Though she doubted a little, still she sang, "Ra-wen-io, I am glad I am going to be like the sky."

"Are you sure that you will be like the sky?" asked a deep voice.

"I am sure," she answered, "for Ra-wen-io, the All-Wise One, has spoken."

"I am Ra-wen-io," said the voice. "Dip in the water once more and touch nothing at all but the water. Then fly upward and sing, 'I have been touched by the brush that colored the sky.' "

With great eagerness Jenny-er-ye flung herself into the water and far down did she dive. When she came to the surface, she was quite out of breath and too tired to fly. She staggered through the ripples to the shore and brushed her breast against the red clay bank, rested a moment, and then flew upward into the warm breeze blowing above the tops of the trees.

The whir of her wings dried her feathers, and as she sang, she noticed the sky's own color had been magically transferred to her feathery coat.

Her joy was a wonderful joy. With a happy heart she sang, "I have been touched by the brush that colored the sky! Great Ra-wen-io has made me beautiful like the sky. I thank him, I thank him, for what I desired he gave me. I thank him."

Then was Ra-wen-io glad he had turned Jenny-er-ye into the first bluebird.

He said to her, "Jenny-er-ye, your coat is blue, but your breast is red. You touched the clay when you came from the water, and though you have the magic of the sky upon your wings, you also have the touch of earth upon your breast. It is well, for in you the sky-world and the earth-world meet. Go your way and sing, and your song will be a sweet thanks to me, Jenny-er-ye!"

Now on a certain morning, O nephew, when

Bluebird was singing "I have been touched by the brush that colored the sky," a cross gray wolf, called Ta-yo-ne, scampered by. He stopped and listened.

"Ho ho," said he, "here is wisdom. Ho ho, if I can be touched by the brush that colored the sky, I shall no longer be gray. And if I become as the sky, I shall then make all the fur folk envious. Ha ha!"

Looking up at Bluebird, Ta-yo-ne called: "Kwey, Sky-Back! How did you find the magic that made you so like the sky?"

Bluebird eagerly told Gray Wolf how he should bathe and how he should sing. She warned him not to touch anything until he was dry, but to sit on the boulder on the shore and sing and sing and sing a very thankful sort of song.

Gray Wolf took a bath every morning. Oh, the water was cold, and when he sang, it sounded like the long drawn-out howl of a dying coyote. But we mustn't laugh. That was his way of singing, O nephew.

On the fourth morning when Gray Wolf trotted ashore, he saw to his astonishment that he was dyed from the tip of his nose to the tip of his tail a beautiful sky-blue. He let out another howl and another and another.

"Woof, how-ow-ow-owo-oooow-wow!" he called.

Turning round and round, he looked himself over. Sure enough, nephew, he was as blue as ever was blue. This made him proud—so proud that he scampered and danced and leaped and twisted and rolled.

He began to think that all the animals from Ga-no na to O-ne-a gah-rah should see him and envy him and wonder at him for his magic.

Ho ho, nephew, learn a thing or two now!

Gray-Wolf-turned-to-Blue-Wolf started a mad rush down the dusty trail. Oh, how he ran, throwing up sticks and stones and dust and more dust as he scampered away.

He had a song, too. Listen, it went this way:

Everybody come, everybody come
And look at me!
How handsome am I, how handsome am I!
Come see, come see!

All the fur folk came down to the trail and watched Ta-yo-ne run to the great meeting place in the big woods. They looked at him and ran alongside of him, and looked at him and ran alongside him, and listened to him—and thought him crazy.

When he reached the council grounds of the fur folk, he mounted a rock and barked out, "Everybody look at me! I have been touched by the brush that colored the sky!"

Everybody did look, and they kept on looking. Then they laughed and kept on laughing. By and by, Ta-yo-ne looked at himself, and he looked again, and kept on looking. He came down from his rock and rolled over, inspecting himself.

He let out a long, dismal howl and slunk away into the swamp. He was gray, as gray as the dust on the trail. There was no trace of blue, not even the faintest trace of blue. His magic was gone, and he skulked away into the boggy thicket, surly and wild.

Now, nephew, this is what happened: Ta-yo-ne was too eager to have praise for his new coat. He did not wait for his gift to dry, and he forgot who gave it to him. He only thought "How handsome am I." When he ran so quickly with his fur all wet, the dust of the trail settled down upon him and covered all he had gained. He was just as gray as ever.

But Bluebird is still blue and happy and her song goes clear up to the sky. Her magic is good, and if you try it, nephew, you'll find that it lasts forever and ever. That's all.

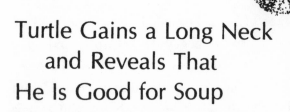

Turtle Gains a Long Neck and Reveals That He Is Good for Soup

YE-HEY, YE-HEY, NEPHEW, NEPHEW! MAYBE SOME-thing is going to happen. Listen!

Oh, Turtle is very old. Long time ago, I told you the green earth rests upon the most ancient of all turtles.

Many winters ago, long before my great-grandfather was born, there was a deep forest hidden away by mountains. In the very middle of that forest was a mossy-banked pond that was fast becoming an oozy bog. In that pond in the middle of the forest was a mossy log, and on that log was the second-cousin-on-his-mother's-side of the great-grandfather of the whole turtle tribe.

Oh, he was a proud old turtle, so the old folk say.

Hah-no-wah—that's the turtle—crawled on the mossy log. He looked very proud and he looked very wise and he looked very dignified.

He was very wise because he was very old. He

was very proud because he was a member of a very old family. And he was very dignified because this was becoming to proud and wise members of very old families.

Turtle was very proper, and everything he did was copied by all other turtles because *he* was *so* proper. But the queer thing about Turtle was that whatever happened to him or any other member of his family, happened to all. So it is that every Turtle looks like all of his kin.

I just said that Turtle was on a mossy log in the pond that lay in the very middle of a forest hidden by mountains. What did Turtle do but look around. He looked down at the scum on his pool. He looked out at the shore where he saw Skoak, the bullfrog, talking to the pollywogs. Then he looked up at Always-Green-Five-Fingers, the pine.

There was something in the pine that attracted his attention. He looked and saw Cross Bill picking seeds from the pine cones that dangled there. Then he looked down in the bushes and saw Whiskered-Fat-Face, the bobcat, talking to Sucks-His-Thumb, the little black bear.

Turtle listened to the conversation and found that Bobcat was talking about him—Turtle. Bullfrog overheard and laughed, "Sko-aak!"

Turtle now thought *he* should say something, so he drawled out, "I am Turtle. The world knows *me*.

I am very wise and very proud, and *I* have a right to be."

At this, Bobcat and Black Bear laughed in their style, and the bird in the tree made a queer sound as if choking on a seed. Bullfrog, too, laughed in his style—"Sko-aak!"

"Oh, Grandfather," called Bobcat, as if to answer Turtle, "see little feathered sister up in the tree picking out seeds?"

Turtle looked up and said, "I have given a wink that way, but for what wisdom?"

"Just this," answered Bobcat. "I can climb trees, Little Bear can sleep inside trees, and the little feathered sister can fly up through the trees and pick a dinner off the end of a cone. Oh, Grandfather, can you do any of these things? Until you can, you shouldn't boast about your old family."

"You have whiskers on your ears," sneered old Turtle.

"So you want to call names?" inquired Bobcat. "Very well, I am going to call you mud-wallower, leech-roost, dead-fish-eater."

"It is not for me to answer green saplings," said Turtle. "I am a man of *dignity* and come from an *old* family."

Just then Bullfrog croaked out, "Sko-aak, sko-aak, sko-aak," very loudly. And if there was one thing above another that Turtle did not like, it was Bull-

frog's commonplace voice. Besides, in the Turtle language, that word "sko-aak" is a swear word. Ho ho,
nephew, you'll listen now!

Hah-no-wah, the Turtle, now was mad. He was
moved to do something desperate. When he got mad,
he forgot something important. He forgot that he
was Turtle, and he forgot that he came from an *old*
family, and he forgot his *dignity*.

Turtle could not endure a challenge. He tried
to swim ashore like Bullfrog. He tried to make a yell
like Bobcat, and he tried to climb a tree like Bear.
His queer antics made all the bugs come out of their
burrows and watch in their rude way.

When Turtle tried to climb the pine, he fell back
forty-eight times plus one. Then he remembered to
rub Swagum, the sacred charm, on his feet. When he
remembered this, he walked up that tree like a bum-
bly bee walks up your face to sting your nose when
you've been smelling a flower. Ho ho!

Up went Turtle, up he went, and up he went, to
the very top of the tree. Then out he went, and out
he went, and out he went, to the tip of the topmost
branch.

There, on the end of the branch, was a pine cone,
and in that cone were seeds.

So far, all was victory for Turtle, and all the
animals but Bullfrog held their breaths.

Turtle now made one wild grab for the pine cone

to get a seed, just like a bird, all because Bobcat had made fun of him. *But*—just as he grabbed, Bullfrog said in his deepest bass, "Sko-aak, sko-aak!"

Sure enough, Turtle caught the cone in his beak. But he was so mad that he wanted to talk—and he did talk. He opened his mouth, and then he lost his balance, and when he lost that, he lost his footing. And when he lost that, over he went in an awkward nose dive straight for the sticky clay below.

Down he fell, down he fell, down he fell, and if the tree had been tall enough, he would be falling yet, but the tree wasn't tall enough. Every fall must have its end, and Turtle found the end of his all too soon. He hit the sticky clay with his nose, and in went his head. Ugh! He was ready to say something, but he couldn't.

Turtle couldn't pull his head out of the clay. He wriggled and twisted and squirmed, but without avail. The more he pulled, the longer his neck grew. He tried to do a handspring, but even this did not loosen the grip of the clay.

Turtle became angry. He was terribly mad, and the madder he got, the more he perspired. He was covered with sweat and boiling with rage. He boiled, and he boiled, and he boiled, until all the woods smelled like turtle soup! All the hungry wood folk sniffed the smell and came to see who was cooking a feast.

After awhile little **Black Bear** thought he would help poor brother Turtle. He playfully grasped Turtle by the shell and pulled. But, oh, what a pull it was! He pulled so long that Turtle's neck stretched out like a black beech pole. Then out snapped turtle's head, flop! and back went his neck, but it never was nice and short again.

This wasn't all. Turtle was so mad and so boiling with rage that he lay steaming and fuming in righteous indignation—and meanwhile the whole world discovered that a turtle boiled long enough makes good soup.

Because of Turtle's escapade, all the other turtles had long necks. None of them knew how it happened, for, bang! they all suddenly got mad and all suddenly found themselves with long necks. And more than this, nephew, every turtle that gets mad is fit for soup.

Now this is what my great-grandfather told me. He was very wise and fought in many wars. He had only one eye, but he saw a lot with that. That's all, nephew!

How the Conifers Flaunt
the Promise of Spring

IN THE MYSTERIOUS DAYS OF LONG AGO, WHEN Ra-wen-io was fixing the earth so that mankind might have a happy place to live, all the trees had tongues and they talked.

There was much to talk about, for terrible monsters roamed the world. None was so terrible as the stern warriors of Winter: Hadui, the storm wind, Hatoe, the frost god, and Gwenny-Oyent, the whirlwind.

These monsters fought the trees and tried to tear them to bits because the trees loved Sun and his friends, Zephyr and Thaw, the kind chiefs of Spring.

The first rumblings of Winter's storms brought the command that all the trees should drop their leaves so that there might remain no track, trace, or remembrance Spring once ruled the year.

To make obedience more difficult, Frost made Autumn paint the leaves with handsome colors so that the trees would hate to drop them. Hadui would come then and pluck every leaf from every tree.

"No friend of Spring shall remain to flaunt his green robes in my face," shrieked Winter, as he drove Hadui against the forest. And Hadui always did his duty.

Winter roared when he saw all the trees bleak and bare. "Ho ho," he bellowed, "the world obeys me and sleeps at my command. Sun has no friends to greet him. Spring is banished, and no sign remains to promise his return. Ho ho, Spring has no friends!"

"I am the friend of Spring," spoke up White Pine.

"That may be," answered Winter, "but when I give the order, away will go your green leaves, and I shall cover them with snow."

"We'll see," said White Pine.

White Pine called a council of all of his tribe, the wonderful tribe of Onetta, the tribe with beautiful green hair.

"Who will stand with me as Winter comes?" called out Pine. "Who will defy Winter and stand his blasts? Who as a friend of Spring will stand as an eternal promise that Spring will return?"

"I will," said Red Pine.

"I will," said Red Cedar.

"I will," said Cypress.

"I will," said Juniper.

"I will," said Hemlock.

"I will," said Spruce.

"I will," said Balsam.

"Where is Tamarack?" shouted Pine.

From a distant hill came a shout, and Tamarack called out, "Oak wants to come to our council, but he is not of our tribe. He wants the hill, and I want the hill."

"Will you defy the Winter god?" called out Pine.

"Yes, I will," answered Tamarack, "but I must finish my argument with Oak first."

Then spoke Oak: "O Pine, I am not of your tribe, for I have broad leaves, but I am a friend of the Sun, of Zephyr, and of Spring. I will stand on the hill and defy the Winter's blasts, and I will rattle my leaves in his face."

Well did all the trees know that Winter hated the sound of rustling leaves, and well did they know the friendship of Oak for Pine.

Whenever Pine went away from a hill, up sprang Oak. And when Oak went away, up sprang Pine. Now Oak would be an ally of the Onetta tribe. Pine said it should be so, but Tamarack was jealous.

"Oak cannot endure," sneered Tamarack. "Oak will yield to Hadui at the first demand."

"I promise to hold my leaves, come what may," answered Oak with a sturdy tone in his voice. "I shall hold them, brown and torn though they may be, until new buds appear."

"Fie," said Tamarack. "Watch me."

Autumn came and at the first demand of Frost, Oak turned a brilliant scarlet. The Onetta tribe refused to obey. Hadui brought rain and then cold, but none faltered save Tamarack who, because he had been envious, had forgotten to drink deep of the magic oil that kept green the rest of the tribe.

Tamarack began to shed his hair and then shed more, for Hadui was cruel and insisted with his lash of storm whips. Oak, however, held onto his leaves, now dry and sear.

"Off with those leaves!" shouted Hadui as Frost swooped down.

But Oak only rattled his leaves in the very face of Frost. Frost grew angry indeed and spent his fury on Pine and his friends, Hemlock and the rest.

Frost chilled the air. He chilled the ground. He chilled the water, and he chilled the trunks of the trees until they resounded to the strokes of his war club when he struck them—hock, hock!

"Off with the promise of Spring," shrieked Frost. But only Tamarack of all the Onetta obeyed and lifted his head and body bare to the wind. Like the drop-leaf trees, he was stripped and naked, which made Frost laugh long and loud.

"Have courage, be strong," called out old Pine.

"Let us endure, though Tamarack has yielded."

And the trees all called out, "We are brave and we are strong. Frost shall not blight the promise of Spring's return."

The gods of Winter ruled long and harshly, holding the earth in cold embrace. But they could not

overcome Pine and his friends. Oak rattled in the face of Frost, and his rustling leaves made Frost wild with rage. And so all endured, except Tamarack.

Round and round went the Moon. It grew full and waned five times before Spring conquered Winter and sent Frost and his evil allies back to the Northland.

The warmth of Sun returned, and with this came Zephyr, who fanned the weary branches of the Onetta tribe back into the glow of growth. Sun warmed Oak and, rustling his leaves, though all dry and frayed, he prepared his new buds.

At length Tamarack awoke and blossomed forth. The tall old Pine looked down at Tamarack and said, "Tamarack, you weakened in the storm, you obeyed the Frost. You are the coward tree and shall dwell in the swamps. You are a vain braggart and have lost the hill. The hill is for Oak, our friend who held onto his leaves and rustled them in the face of the storm."

Tamarack begged for the hill, where he might be admired by all for his long plumes and graceful wave when Zephyr tossed his branches, but old Pine would not hear.

And so, forever afterward, the kinsmen of Pine hold forth the promise of Spring's return, and their green robes are the despair of Winter and all his furious hosts.

The Turtle's War Party

HAIL, NEPHEW, HAIL! MY POUCH OF MAGIC TALES IS open. Listen to the tale of Turtle and how he would be chief.

Long ago in the world of Used-to-be, this was, and Turtle was there. He was on a mossy log in a green, scummy lake when he heard Hoot Owl and Bobcat disputing.

"Hoot, hoot, hoot!" exclaimed Hoot Owl. "Turtle is no man. He never led a band of warriors. He is a coward, I tell you!"

"Coward, coward? Not at all, for I saw him pluck the eye from a dead fish. He is brave, is brave. Turtle can fight dead frogs," said Bobcat.

Bobcat then looked slyly at Turtle on his log, but Hoot Owl only flew to a swamp stub and mocked back, "Hoot, hoot! Turtle is no man!"

Turtle thereupon became very angry and made

up his mind after four days of anger to call for warriors and make a raid on Huk-sah, the Jungie who
threw stones at him. Ah, he would kill Huk-sah and
his whole family, too.

Slowly Turtle swam down the little stream that
drained the swamp where lay the lake. He came to
a swift river. Here he prowled about for a time looking for good fortune. At length he discovered it in
the form of Huk-sah's canoe. Here was a prize
worthy of a chief of warriors.

Turtle now devised a war song which by its
power would attract brave fighters. After four days
of thinking he had his song, and in triumph he sang:

> Warriors bold where e'er you be,
> Come along and fight for me.
> Come along and fight like me,
> Fight and bite, but never flee.

Singing his song, Turtle seized a paddle and
pushed the canoe far out into the stream. Long and
loud he sang, hoping to attract brave men.

Fox heard the challenge to war and barked out
over the water. "I'll join, I'll join," he yelped.

Turtle paddled ashore and shouted, "Show me
what you can do."

Fox danced around and then ran with great
swiftness into the forest. Then he came back for the
verdict.

"Don't want you," said Turtle. "You are too swift. You might fight and bite, but you would run away." So saying, Turtle paddled on.

Rattlesnake, sunning himself on a rock, heard and gave a great hiss that sounded over the river.

Turtle paddled ashore and shouted, "Come on, Black Face, show me what you can do."

Rattlesnake coiled and sprang at a rabbit hiding in a brush pile. The rabbit quivered and died.

"Jump in," called out Turtle in glee, for he had his first recruit.

When Rattlesnake leaped in, Turtle paddled on, singing even more gleefully his challenge song.

Dog, hearing the invitation to war, howled his answer over the water and Turtle paddled ashore.

"Show me what you can do," called Turtle.

Dog barked and scampered about. But when a nut fell from a tree, he put his tail between his legs and ran so fast Turtle could not see where Dog went.

Turtle crawled back into his canoe and paddled on, singing his song of war.

Porcupine, ambling through the underbrush, heard the call to war and whistled his answer.

Turtle came ashore and called, "What can you do, Needle Feathers?"

Porcupine just shook himself and threw his poisoned arrows right and left.

"Jump in," said Turtle, for he liked warriors

who took their time and did not run.

Down the stream went the three, Turtle singing as he paddled.

Presently Sayno, the skunk, heard the song and called out over the river.

Turtle came ashore and asked, "What can you do, Bushy-Tailed White-Stripe?"

Skunk just looked at Turtle very sorrowfully, and Turtle knew what Skunk could do, so he said, "Jump in!" He liked warriors who took their time and did not run.

Turtle sang all day, but not another warrior did he find who would go with him, though he liked Panther, Fisher, and Wolverine. But they would not join him when they saw his allies, and neither would Horned Owl and Buzzard.

Turtle now neared the lodge of his enemy, Huksah. He took the canoe ashore and drew up his warriors.

"Oh, you of the black face," he said to Rattlesnake, "you hide in the basket of wood and strike the hand that touches it."

Turtle, you see, planned to surround the lodge so that no one could escape.

"Now you of the needle feathers, you climb upon the roof, and when your colleague strikes, you shake your darts down the smoke hole and put out the eyes of the Jungies inside."

Looking about, he sought to find a place for Skunk. At last he spied the back door of the lodge and ordered Skunk to take his station there.

Turtle now wondered where he should hide for his part in the fray and after wandering about found a spring. Into its depths he dived, safe and secure.

Now it was only a matter of waiting for the attack. Dawn came, and the inmates of the lodge awakened. The enemy was ready to strike.

Huk-sah's mother came out for her kindling, and as she did so, she saw a glitter in the basket.

"Ah-gey," she exclaimed, "there is a snake here," and, so saying, she struck Rattlesnake with her corn pestle before he could even coil for a strike.

Huk-sah now sprang to his feet and looked out the rear door, for he detected an odd odor seeping in through the bark sides of the house.

"Ho ho!" he exclaimed. "I see him," and, taking his bow, he fixed an arrow and shot Skunk.

The mother now came into the lodge and, looking into the kettle of oil in the fireplace under the smoke hole, she saw Porcupine peering down. Quickly she threw a handful of tobacco into the embers. It sent up such a smudge that Porcupine was bewildered and tumbled down into the kettle and drowned.

Huk-sah's father now went down to the spring for a bark bucket of water. As he sank the bucket's rim beneath the surface of the spring, Turtle grasped his leg with a terrible bite.

"Ah-gey!" yelled the warrior, taken by surprise. Then he looked down and saw Turtle. "Ho ho," he exclaimed, "Turtle is here for a fight. Well, I will fight him! I'll thrust him in the fire!"

Turtle was thoroughly frightened. He knew all his allies were dead, so he said, "Oh, please put me in the fire so I may recover my power. Fire I love, fire I breathe, fire I drink. Ho ho!"

"If you love fire so well, I will fling you far from it," said Huk-sah's father. "I will drown you in the river."

"No, no!" begged Turtle. "Put me not in the water, for if you do I shall surely die."

So, as quickly as he could limp to the river, Huk-sah's father thrust Turtle into the water. Turtle, letting go the Jungie's leg, sank slowly to the bottom of the stream. There he remained four days.

After awhile Turtle arose and crawled up on the sun-warmed riverbank. For four days he thought about himself. Finally he crawled away to his own pond, where he found safety on his slimy log.

"I was not meant for a chief," he muttered. "My war party failed, and for all generations to come I shall be hunted by men-beings. Ah-gey, war is not for me."

Ho ho, nephew, that is what Turtle said. That's all.

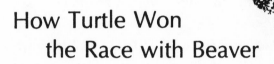

How Turtle Won
the Race with Beaver

THERE WAS A MOSSY-BANKED POND IN A GREAT thicket of thorns in the land of Used-to-Be. In that pond was a slimy log with a flat end, and this was Hah-no-wah's sun parlor. Ye-hey, nephew, this is a story of Hah-no-wah, the Turtle. Listen!

Up climbed Hah-no-wah. He felt very sluggish, and as he lay upon the log he shivered, for no sun came to shine upon him, and no warm wind fanned his cold, wet sides.

Hah-no-wah felt disgusted and made up his mind—after four days of disgust—to retire to his underwater lodgings.

His house under water was beneath a shelving rock. It was packed with water moss and decaying wood. This was luxury to Hah-no-wah, for moss and old wood were fine furniture to his way of thinking. Ho ho, nephew, now something is going to happen.

Hah-no-wah inspected his lodge and then crept up above the water to inspect the world. It was all his world because the pond was small and the thicket of thorns kept prowlers away. He was an ancient resident, and newcomers were not welcome.

The thicket looked strong, the pond looked stagnant, and all seemed safe to Hah-no-wah, so he slid from his sun parlor and plopped into the green water beneath whose scum was his lodging, filled with water moss and decaying wood. In he went and closed the door.

The time had come for his winter sleep. Hah-no-wah loved to sleep, and he loved to dream of the old days when there were only turtles in the world and no newcomers to be kept away with thorn thickets.

Long slept Hah-no-wah, and sweet were his dreams. He was a hero, he was a hunter, and behold, he was Chief. The whole world was his, and only he could enjoy the warmth of the sun.

Long Turtle slept beneath the shelving rock upon his bed of moss and decaying wood. Then something stirred within him and he began to awaken.

For four days he moved a little and tried to go to sleep again, but even a turtle must awaken. So Hah-no-wah crawled out of bed and opened his chamber door. He looked up, and the water seemed clearer than ever before. He gave a slight jump.

He gave another jump, and still another, and still four more. He came to the surface and looked for his log. It was not there. He looked for the bank of his pond, and it was not there. He looked, and everywhere he saw only water running far into the thicket of thorns.

Mullets and catfish swam about him, suckers and pollywogs sported in the pond beside him. Then he saw a furry back swimming toward a big round mound.

Hah-no-wah was startled. His pond had grown to a great lake that covered the thicket.

He made up his mind to explore his enlarged domain. He began a slow, dignified water-crawl until at length he came to a row of logs, forming a dam.

"Confusion!" he snorted. "A newcomer has been here. A newcomer has erected an obstruction, enlarging my pond and taking possession while I slept. Shall I submit? No, I shall not."

In a high dudgeon, Hah-no-wah swam back from the dam and swam and swam until he came to the big round mound of sticks and cattails. He crawled up on it and thumped it with his chest.

Out came a furry newcomer to see who was knocking on his roof.

"Hai-ee, Furry-newer," called Hah-no-wah. "What are you doing in *my* pond? Who gave *you* permission to enlarge my waters and make them clear? Who told you to build an obstruction?"

"Hai-ee, Moss-backed-sleeper," said the furry stranger. "My name is Beaver and I go where I like.

I love to work, and if other creatures want to get along with me they had best let me alone." And slap, slap, slap, went Beaver's flat tail upon the water, making a noise like the clapping of hands.

"It's my pond, I tell you," screamed Turtle.

"It used to be," barked back Beaver.

"It's mine yet, I tell you," yelled Turtle.

"Well, let's agree to live together in peace," suggested Beaver, trying to be friendly. "There is enough room for all who want to live here."

"Not room for you," snapped Turtle. "You get out or I'll break down your dam."

"I'll build another, and all my sons will build more and more and more until you break your neck trying to break my logs," said Beaver.

"Then here is where we fight," said Turtle.

"All right," said Beaver. "Let it be a contest. We will dive, and the one who first brings up mud from the bottom will win."

Down they both dived and up they both came at the same moment with a mouthful of mud.

"We are even," said Beaver. "What shall we now do? I suggest a race from the dam to the great rock at the upper end of the stream. Who so wins shall own the pond and he shall be Chief."

"Let's go," said Turtle. "To this I agree."

Beaver swiftly forged ahead, and when Turtle saw how swiftly Beaver swam, he called out, "No, no,

I am not ready yet. Let us get together, tail to tail. When I nip your tail, then you start. When I nip again, stop."

The race started over again, Turtle pinching the Beaver's tail as a signal. Off they went. Ho ho, nephew, Turtle is cunning.

When Hah-no-wah bit Beaver's tail, he did not let go, but let Beaver tow him far up the pond and within sight of the big rock at the head of the stream. Beaver never knew that Turtle had used stealth.

Beaver approached the goal, feeling he would win, for Turtle was not yet ahead. So he thought, nephew, but he didn't think hard enough, for just then Turtle bit deep and viciously.

"Ug-gee," snorted Beaver, convulsed with pain and flinging his wounded tail over his head. It was uncommonly heavy, for Turtle held fast and only let go when in midair.

Swish Turtle went, thrown by the jerk of Beaver's tail. *Plop* he went upon the ground far ashore.

Safe on the bank, he called out, "*Kwey,* Furry-newer, *kwey,* are you yet in sight? I've been here a long time. Where are you? I am shouting as winner. I have won the race!"

Beaver looked up, and sure enough there sat Turtle at the base of the big rock.

"You have won, indeed," said Beaver, "but I

cannot remember seeing you pass me. You must be very swift. The pond is yours, and you may call it yours, but I shall stay there, too, and we shall be neighbors."

"Waugh!" snorted Turtle. "Such neighbors!"

Beaver slapped his sore tail upon the water, and as he did, a school of minnows darted by, and salamanders and spiders and water bugs skimmed over the water. Turtle looked long and hard at these new neighbors and figured out that here was meat to eat, more meat than he had ever seen before.

He looked at the banks of the pond and saw long timbers of decayed wood covered with moss, more timbers and more moss than he had ever seen before. And there to one side was a wide stretch of sandy ground where the sun beat down hot.

It looked good to him—this world of which he was Chief, and so he said to Beaver, "You go back to your mound. As I have won this race fairly, I am Chief."

"Nyuh," said Beaver, "you are Chief, indeed. Be that as it is, I am worker, builder, channel maker. Where I go, there the ponds grow larger and life is more abuandant."

And so it was, nephew, that Turtle won the race and Beaver got a sore tail, and it's been that way ever since, so the old folk say. Ho ho, nephew, that's all.

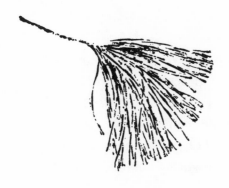

Turtle Runs a Race with Bear

TURTLE KNEW TWO THINGS: HE KNEW THAT HE was very wise and he knew that he was very slow. Nevertheless, Turtle had a certain advantage over other four-foots. It lay in the fact that there were so many turtles. So now the story.

Along came Bear with an ambling gait. He jumped over a log in a comical fashion and then stopped as Turtle Warrior challenged him.

"What are you doing here?" asked Turtle Warrior. "Don't you know better than to come into the domain of Turtle Chief without asking permission?"

"Oh, so Turtle is Chief here?" asked Bear. "I didn't know that."

"Better go to his wigwam and tell why you have come here," said Turtle Warrior.

"All right, I will," answered Bear, with a gleam in his eye.

Away he went to the wigwam of Turtle Chief. After he had smoked a peace pipe and talked about wet weather and why hazelnuts are full of meat, he began to tell why he had come.

"I'd like to be Chief here," announced Bear.

"You will have to win by contest," said Turtle Chief.

"What shall we do?" asked Bear.

"Dive and he who comes up last wins," said Turtle Chief with a grin.

"No," replied Bear, "let us run a race."

Turtle scratched his left ear, and then he scratched his right knee, and then he smoked his pipe thoughtfully, all the while saying, "Nuh, nuh, nuh, nyuh!"

After awhile Turtle Chief said, "It is well known, O Bear, that I, Turtle Chief, am a swift runner. It is scarcely honorable for me to race with you, for I would surely win."

Bear-Who-Would-Be-Chief looked at Turtle Chief with a smile. "Well," said he slowly, rubbing his nose with his paw, "I can no more than lose."

"Precisely so," answered Turtle Chief.

"Let's start," suggested Bear.

"In due time," said Turtle Chief. "But you know that I have much to lose if I lose. What will you lose if you lose?"

"Oh," answered Bear, "you mean that I should

put up a big present for you in case I lose?"

"Precisely so," said Turtle Chief, with a twist of his tail.

"Well, just to show that I mean business and am no impostor, I will place twenty wampum belts, forty canoes, sixty toboggans, a hundred pipe pouches, all well quilled, and two hundred baskets of honey, five hundred strings of beads, and a thousand dried fish, also a fine comb carved of elk horn."

"What do I want with a comb?" snapped Turtle. "You can leave that out. You may need it yourself."

"When do we start?" asked Bear.

"Start?" echoed Turtle Chief. "Oh, yes, we start when the wind blows, when the snow flurries, when the cold comes, when the ice is upon the river."

"Why wait?" inquired Bear. "Cold time is my sleepy time."

"It's the only time we can run upon the river," answered Turtle Chief. "You see, you will run upon the ice, and I will swim under it. Our goal will be the other side."

"Suits me," said Bear, thinking all the time he could win, even though half asleep.

"Go get your pledge goods," said Turtle Chief, and Bear, though he disliked to carry big loads, ambled off for his pledges, believing that after all he would soon own all the land and have his den in the cliff that rose back of the woods.

Turtle Chief began to get busy. He called all the other turtles of his tribe and selected two dozen and six who looked just like him.

Said Turtle Chief, "My tribesmen, a bothersome bear seeks to make his home here by the river. He wishes to run a race with me, and I must win. When the ice covers the river, I will make thirty holes in it. One of you must station himself at each hole and look out. When you see Bear coming, you must say, 'Ho, Bear! Hi, Bear! I have been here a long time waiting for you to catch up.' Then you must duck under and go to bed."

Turtle Chief planned well and fixed his post on the opposite shore. Along came Bear when the ice was two fingers thick. Turtle Warrior announced the race course was ready and Turtle Chief was in his wigwam waiting.

Bear went to the wigwam and greeted Turtle Chief.

"Now," said Turtle Chief, "I will go into the water and see if all is ready beneath the ice. You start straight across when my Warrior gives the signal."

Of course Bear agreed, and when Turtle Chief had inspected the great heaps of pledges, he dived under the water and was gone a long time. After awhile, Turtle Warrior gave the signal. Yawning, Bear started off with a loping gait.

Soon he came to a hole in the ice where he saw Turtle's head sticking out.

"Ho, Bear! Hi, Bear! I have been here a long time waiting for you to catch up," shouted Turtle, ducking under.

Bear was amazed, but trotted on faster and faster. Soon he came to another hole where Turtle awaited him with a "Ho, Bear! Hi, Bear!"

Bear was now frightened at Turtle's speed, and summoning up all his speed, ran on, only to come to another hole and find Turtle waiting for him.

Again and again he saw Turtle looking out from his hole. Madly Bear ran and ran and ran. Finally, with that mocking call of "Ho, Bear! Hi, Bear!" ringing in his ears, he reached the farther bank of the river, where Turtle Chief awaited him with a "Ho, Bear! Hi, Bear! I have been waiting here a long time for you to catch up!"

"Oh, I am beaten," panted Bear, his sides heaving with exhaustion. "I didn't know you could run so fast."

"I warned you," said Turtle. "We should have tried diving."

"I've lost the race, I've lost my fortune, I've lost a fine place to live in," moaned Bear, yawning with weariness.

"But you have gained a lot of experience," said Turtle Chief, with a wise look. "You know now that Turtle Chief is swift and that he is Chief here."

"Yes," said Bear.

"And you know that Turtle Chief is very wise," said Turtle Chief.

"Yes," said Bear.

"And you know that it is time for you to hunt a cave and go to bed," said the aggravating victor, smiling as he wriggled his tail.

"Yes," said Bear, ambling off to his cave.

And to this day Bear doesn't know just how he happened to lose that race, but, nephew, we who know that there are many turtles, know how the trick was turned. And, now that we know it, the story is done.

The Grand Sagamore
Who Wandered Afar

ONCE NEAR A HILL, O NEPHEW, THERE WAS A ROCKY dell, and in that dell was a cliff, and in that cliff were a lot of holes.

Now holes may amount to something or they may not, but these did. They were the front doors of the Grand Sagamoredom of Sleek Cheek, Grand Sagamore of Gray Wolves. Yes, nephew, wolves lived there.

Upon a certain day the wolves held a special dance in honor of Sleek Cheek, the young wolf who because of his royaneh, or noble, birth was to become the new Grand Sagamore of the Gray Wolves. All the great wolves made speeches and presented much wampum to Sleek Cheek because the Gray Wolves needed a strong new Sagamore, or chief.

And it must be said that Sleek Cheek was a fine fellow. Everybody loved him. He was as smart as a fox in a duck's bedroom. He was also handsome to

see, and smart, too. That was lucky for the Gray
Wolves, and they were very proud their Grand Sagamore was the descendant of an ancient line.

No man was better fitted than he to run the
affairs of the tribe. But Sleek Cheek was a rover by
nature, and after he had been Grand Sagamore for
a moon and a half, he wanted to travel and see the
world—and also to tell the world he was Grand Sagamore back home.

Proudly the whole tribe bade him good-bye and
luck on his journey.

"Mighty fine people," he thought. "I don't know
how they will get along when I am away. Still, a
Grand Sagamore must see the world."

Many countries did Sleek Cheek see, and many
feasts did he attend. Each Grand Sagamoredom
wherever he went did him grand honors. He grew
fat and satisfied with himself. Ah, he was Grand
Sagamore!

Now the tribe at home began to have a hard
time, just as Sleek Cheek hoped. He knew that this
would make his fellow wolves appreciate who he was.

A hungry time came when the little gray wolves
cried for food. Food was scarce and the hunting
ground far away. Winter came and food grew scarcer,
so much so that these proud people were forced to
eat wood mice and dead partridges.

After awhile, Rough Fellow began to grumble

around. After awhile, he called a council.

"Come on, you fellows," he said. "We must dig out of here and scurry up some grub."

The refined gray wolves were shocked at this sort of a speech and said, "No, no. We will await our Grand Sagamore. He shall lead us."

"If you wait for him, the crows will eat you for breakfast some fine morning," said Rough Fellow. "Come on, now, follow me, and I'll take you to a place where the deer are thick. What's so fine as good deer meat?"

"Deer meat!" they all exclaimed. "How good that would taste."

"All right," said an old mother wolf. "Lead us to meat. We are hungry, and the babies are crying."

"You have got to do as I say then," said Rough Fellow.

"All right," they said, nice folks and all. "Only give us meat."

So off they went, following their leader and yelping after meat. They found a lot of deer wallowing in the snow, and after a glorious battle they killed enough meat for a whole moon. They stayed there and had a feast.

When they had filled themselves, Rough Fellow said, "I am boss around here now. You follow me."

So they followed Rough Fellow until they came to a buffalo herd stamping around in the snow. Here was the gray wolves' favorite food, but it would take a fight to overcome the herd.

Rough Fellow said, "Now, you folks just follow me and I'll show you!"

He bossed them around and showed them how to make an attack. They charged. Oh, what a glorious fight it was! A whole lot of buffaloes lay there on the snow, and only one man was wounded among all the gray wolves.

Again the gray wolves feasted and became stronger and bolder. There was only one hitch now. Every time anything was killed, no wolf dared take a bite until Rough Fellow had his fill. He got all the choice steaks. When he finished his meal, the rest could have what was left.

Certain wolves didn't like such selfish actions and said so to Rough Fellow. But he rushed at them and grabbed them by the throats and broke their necks in a jiffy. No man could tell him what to do! Thus perished a good half-dozen noble wolves who loved to see things done decently.

Winter passed and spring came. It was time for the cliff and the holes again. So back they went, fat and contented with everything, except for the fact that Rough Fellow was so cross and snappy.

One morning, just as they were getting up, there was a loud signal call from the hill.

"Coming back, coming back!" called a voice.

Out the wolves all rushed and there, galloping toward them, was their own Grand Sagamore, Sleek Cheek.

"I am back now," he called, "and we shall have a council."

The council met around a tall tree and Sleek Cheek told of his adventures.

"Now," said he, "we shall travel far over the hills to a new rocky dell where we have many friends. I want them to see how you honor me and obey my orders."

"What's that?" snapped a rough voice. It was Rough Fellow speaking, and he was pretty mad, too. "Who spoke about orders?"

"I, your Grand Sagamore, spoke of orders," an-

swered Sleek Cheek. "We are going to take a journey."

"Nothing of the kind," roared Rough Fellow.
"This pack obeys me."

Sleek Cheek looked startled. "I am Grand Sagamore," he snorted.

"That may all be true," roared back Rough
Fellow. "You may be Grand Sagamore, but I am
boss."

"Who will follow me?" asked Sleek Cheek.

There was no answer.

"Who will follow me?" yelped Rough Fellow.

"I will," yelled everybody, remembering the
meat hunt.

Rough Fellow laughed as he turned to Sleek
Cheek. "Now you skip along," he ordered. "You can
go where you get your grand honors. But I am going
to stay here and boss this pack."

Sleek Cheek looked at his tribe and said, "Come,
my tribe."

Rough Fellow looked at his fellows and yelped
in a sort of low growl, "Stay, my pack!"

The pack stayed.

Sleek Cheek slunk away at the top of the hill.
That night as the moon came out, the Grand Sagamoredom of Rough Fellow heard a long, piteous
howl.

The Buffalo's Hump
and the Brown Birds

THE GREAT DAY WAS COMING FOR THE RACE TO NEW
fields.

For a long time the Tribe of Buffaloes had been
uneasy. The thunder god had withheld rain from the
prairie lands, and the grass was withered and dead.
The buffaloes needed grass to eat, and now they
stamped and snorted when they smelled rain to the
west. This meant new grass.

The old buffalo chief held back his tribesmen,
saying, "Stay here, for rain will come. Over there in
the west are other herds who have long waited for
rain."

The young buffalo chief would not agree. He
harangued his fellows and roused them to frenzy.

"Come," said he, "let us go where the grass is
green!"

Young Buffalo and Old Buffalo faced each other
with lowered horns, their eyes rolling white with
anger.

"We will not go," said Old Buffalo.

"We will go," said Young Buffalo.

"We shall wrestle, and if you throw me, we shall go," said Old Buffalo. "If I throw you, we shall stay."

Then began the wrestling match. Pressing sharp horns against each other, the two chiefs pushed and twisted, their breath coming fast and faster, their voices bellowing with defiance.

Suddenly Young Buffalo's brother-friend edged out from the herd and gored Old Buffalo from the opposite side. Old Buffalo turned quickly upon his new adversary and roared at him. This gave Young Buffalo a chance to lift Old Buffalo into the air and toss him over upon his back.

A great shout went up. "Tomorrow we go!"

The old chief rose from the ground, anger gleaming in his eyes.

"I will abide by my word," said he, "but treachery like that which tripped me has no reward. If Young Buffalo tricks me, he will trick all of you."

"All's fair in a fight," boasted Young Buffalo.

"Not under the law of the Masterful One," said the older buffalo. "Well do you know that if one of us makes a grave error, all of us suffer."

"Enough of that," shouted the young buffaloes. "Tomorrow we go."

And so the tomorrow came, and with it the excitement of preparation. As was the custom in those days, the winner of the race to new fields would become the grand chief of the herd. All the strong young fellows were prancing and calling upon their magic for power.

In the first light of the morning the vast herd ranged itself for the race. The sun rolled red over the prairie, and this was the signal to start on the race from the sunrise to the sunset. Off they went in high spirits!

"Follow me," called out Old Buffalo, and all the wary buffaloes followed, taking a winding course over the short grass.

"Follow me," called out Young Buffalo, and all the foolish buffaloes followed, taking a straight course through the tall grass.

"Stay with me," called out Brown Buffalo, the smallest fellow in the herd, and all the really wise buffaloes stayed at home with Brown Buffalo, son of Old Buffalo.

"Now," said Brown Buffalo, "we shall abide here and make a herd of our own. Rain will come, and we shall have new grass, just as Old Buffalo said. But he let himself be misled by a challenge. I stay, he goes. We shall see."

So those who stayed at home with Brown Buffalo nibbled dead grass and sweltered in dust.

Far out on the plains rushed the two rival herds,

one taking the straight way through the tall grass, and the other swinging around through the short grass. As they rushed on, the dust flew high and the ground rumbled with the sound of thundering feet.

Young Buffalo knew that he would win, for his course was shorter. He capered through the grass, halting his tribesmen for a wild dance. Around and around they milled, trampling the grass to the earth. Away scampered rabbits, away sped frightened deer, and upward with wild screams flew flocks of brown birds.

Then on over the plains rushed Young Chief and his herd, smashing into grass clumps where birds had nested. Indeed, they sought out such spots just to crush the homes of the birds and rushed on with the sound of wild screeching ringing in their ears.

Overhead swirled homeless flocks of birds, weeping at their loss of nests and young. No love had they for dashing buffalo herds.

Old Buffalo, sticking to the short grass route, found his journey easier. No entanglements or temptations lay in his path. On he rushed with his trampling herd.

The sun rose high and hot. It shone down with merciless heat, its scorching darts making the onrushing herds mad with thirst and exhaustion. Scores perished as they ran, falling to the blistered earth to make feasts for prowling packs of wolves.

Still on rushed the maddened survivors. But the herds grew thinner and thinner, until only Young Buffalo and Old Buffalo remained in the race. From their widely separated paths, each saw the other. Wildly each ran to reach the goal at the place where the sun goes down.

At last their paths merged, and side by side they ran until the sun was a sinking ball on the western horizon.

The sun dropped down and was gone. The rival buffaloes with heaving sides and rolling eyes looked at one another. Each had come to the end of his journey—and all about them was dry grass. Not a green blade of grass was to be seen.

Far to the east, from whence they had come, there was the sound of distant thunder, and then came the smell of rain.

The darkening sky lighted up as a great cloud appeared. From it, clothed in light and beaming with stars, a figure stood out. It was the Masterful One with a spear in his hand. Out of the cloud he came in visible form and descended to earth.

The buffaloes stood in dismay. What could this mean? They waited in awe.

"Oh, foolhardy buffaloes," spoke the Great Voice, "you have slain your herds and there is none to follow you. You sought a land blessed by rich grass. Behold, it is from whence you came, and little Brown

Buffalo is there with his herd. He is chief now and
guides all that remain of your tribe. Step forward
and receive your punishment, that all buffaloes may
remember this day."

The two buffaloes stepped forward, and as they
did, the Masterful One struck them over their
shoulders with his spear. Immediately a great hump
appeared upon each.

"And because you were careless, Young Buffalo,
I shall use you to remind everyone who shall come
after you that it is wrong to destroy the nests of birds.
Why did you trample upon them and leave them
homeless forever?"

"I thought it only sport," answered Young
Buffalo.

"Henceforth you will look where you go," said
the Masterful One. "All buffaloes who are hereafter
born, and all who now live, shall by this token beware."

The Masterful One stepped upon Young Buffalo's head and thrust it down to the ground.

"Look to the lowly ones beneath your feet," said
the Masterful One.

The great being now lifted up his hand and
spoke again.

"Oh, Old Buffalo, you should have been wise,"
he said. "You might have held back your herds, but
you did not. You gave good advice, but you could not

lead. I now transform you into the White Buffalo of the clouds. When the sun is red, you shall appear in the clouds to warn your tribesmen of danger ahead."

So saying, he touched Old Buffalo and immediately he became white and flew away to the night clouds, there to abide forever.

Again the great being lifted his hand and spoke.

"Oh, Young Buffalo, you were impulsive," he said. "You wanted to lead your herd to green grass, but green grass is not here. It is far to the east, where Brown Buffalo leads his herds to safety. You are a destroyer of birds, and henceforth the brown birds shall depend upon buffaloes for food and protection. Your kinsmen far to the east even now find themselves surrounded with brown birds who will live with them hereafter. As for you, I transform you into the Red Buffalo of the under-earth. Be gone!"

Young Buffalo became red and sank into the ground, there to live forever with the monsters who had failed to please the Masterful One.

The next morning, Brown Buffalo in his green pasture found his herd surrounded with friendly brown birds that picked at the grass and flew upon the backs of his tribesmen. And so it is to this day.

Buffaloes have humps, they hang their heads low, and about them are birds that never build nests. How this happened you have learned, and this is the wisdom of the wise men of old. Na ho.

Toad Brother's Warts and the Peeper's Peep

A LONG TIME AGO, WHEN THE GREEN WORLD WAS new, there were some wicked bugs. Now, everyone knows that the wicked bugs have long tried to eat up the world, and it was so from the beginning of time. Whenever a new leaf appeared, bad bugs wanted to eat it. So this is the beginning of our story.

In a pleasant forest grove there was a beautiful garden of plants with lovely flowers, broad leaves, and big roots. These plants shaded the homes of a village of hoppers. One spring morning when strawberries were ripe, all the frogs were excited, for Tree Hopper from his perch saw a whole war party of leaf eaters coming with their allies, the fuzzy crawlers.

No wonder the hoppers were excited—for should these enemies find the beautiful garden, they would eat every bit of it and make a bare spot. The sun would bake the ground and leave only dust for the frogs to live in. And hoppers like plenty of shade.

Strange to relate, in those days the hoppers were afraid of the wicked bugs and always fled from them. But now they determined to fight.

On came the enemy, marching in regular order under their war captains. Oh, what could the hoppers do against such foes that bit and burned where they touched?

The frogs were dismayed, all but Peeper Hopper and Big Mouth Hopper. They stood their ground while all the other hoppers hid under rocks far from the garden.

On came the enemy, and the two faithful hoppers marched out to meet them. These two were sworn friends and never had failed each other. On they hopped toward the foe until they were right against the line of wicked bugs. Then came the fight.

Big Mouth began to slap bugs right and left. Peeper kicked fuzzy crawlers until they rolled in all directions.

How brave were these hoppers in the midst of those wicked bug warriors. But after a time, they began to see the enemy was overwhelming them. They could now hardly move.

All over Peeper crawled the fuzzy crawlers, and all over Big Mouth swarmed the wicked bugs, biting and stinging in a terrible way. Soon the crawlers tied up Peeper in a net of cords and dragged him to a torture stake. Big Mouth shook off the wicked bugs and hopped as fast as he could for a mudhole. Had he deserted his friend? We shall see.

The fuzzy crawlers now gathered their faggots and built a fire. Ah, what a fire it would be, for the torture stake was of fine fat pitch pine and full of rosin. Peeper would suffer now. The foe would hear his peeps as he burned, and the foe would laugh as he peeped.

On the flames crept until they began to bite into Peeper's flesh, but he never peeped. Lucky for him he was on the wrong side of the fire. It fanned against the back of the torture stake and its hot rosin oozed out and dripped behind. Fortune was with him if the fire burned this way, and the foe didn't laugh half as much as planned. Now wait.

Right down on the flame side of the torture stake was Big Mouth, digging a hole as fast as he could so that the stake would fall over and free Peeper. Like fury he dug, and used both mouth and feet to do it. All the while, the hot rosin dripped down on his back, burning him horribly, but he never even cried.

Peeper, meanwhile, kept jumping and jumping and jumping and straining at the stake, until at last it loosened where Big Mouth had dug the ground away. Peeper gave a final struggle and freed himself.

With a mighty jump Peeper scattered the fire all over the wicked bugs and the fuzzy crawlers, burning them to death. Two jumps more took him to the pool in the swamp, and into this Peeper dived, there to cool his blistered shins and parched tummy. He was safe at last and now began to peep for Big Mouth, but Big Mouth was hurt.

Big Mouth was sick, and the sizzling rosin burned deeply into his poor back. It was he who had been tortured, it was he who had been the victim, but he had no strength to jump to the cooling pond. He was too weak, and the fire had gone into his eyes until they bulged and ached. Slowly he crawled under an old log and lay there a long, long time, scarcely breathing. He was sick enough to die.

As he lay there wondering what would become of him, a Jungie, prowling through the underbrush, found Big Mouth and gave him a healing herb which cooled his blistered back.

"I saw what you did to save Peeper," said the Jungie.

"He was my friend," said Big Mouth.

"And I am your friend," said Jungie. "You did a good deed and you saved Peeper."

"He was my friend," said Big Mouth.

"I am your friend," said Jungie. "You are badly burned, and the scars will always remain, but I will give you a magic tongue. With it you can fight all the wicked bugs and the fuzzy crawlers. You have only to stick it out at them, and they will disappear right down your throat."

"What will I do, then?" asked Big Mouth, beginning to get interested.

"Eat 'em up," answered Jungie. "Eat 'em up. As long as you live, you will stay in a green garden and hunt the wicked bugs that caused the blisters on your poor back. And as long as you live, I am your good friend."

Jungie went away, looking for more of his friends. After awhile Big Mouth Hopper hopped out from his hiding place under the log. On his back were many ugly warts, and he was gray where the ashes and embers had fallen on him. In his eyes, too, blazed the fire that he had looked at undaunted. Though his back was stiff and warty, in his mouth was a magic tongue and he was anxious to try it.

Big Mouth hopped right up to a cluster of leaf bugs that were eating a plant in the garden. Like a flash, he unrolled his tongue, and all of them disappeared instantly! They never even saw his tongue. It takes a keen eye to see it, so the wise old people say, and just you try some day.

Big Mouth long wondered where his friend had gone. He looks even yet for him, and many a time he is seen hopping around in the ashes of an old camp fire, seeking for signs of Peeper, whom he last saw in the flames of the torture stake.

While he is looking, Peeper, who is afraid to come on dry land, keeps peeping from his pool and saying, "Oh, Big Mouth, hurry to the water. Peep, peep."

What a fine friend Big Mouth was, and his warts are the badges of his valor. Think how he got them, and, like the good Jungie, always salute Big Mouth and call him friend.

And who is Big Mouth? Can't you guess? Of course you can!

Well, now that you have guessed Big Mouth was Brother Toad, guess again who told the terrible lie that toads give people warts?

Can you guess? No? Well, it was a very wicked bug who wanted to get his revenge. And it is true that many poor toads have been killed by thoughtless people who believed that lie about Brother Toad.

Toad's my friend and he's yours too, and Peeper's your friend, for he tells you spring is coming and with it more wicked bugs.

How Moose and Turkey Scalped the Giants

THERE WAS A GREAT CRASHING OF UNDERBRUSH AND all the animals of the forest bellowed and screeched. The terrible Stone Coats, most horrible of all giants, were roaming about. Except for the soles of their feet, these giants were protected from any fatal injury.

The Stone Coats were tall and mighty, and their hunger was that of twenty bears. They delighted in killing. This the fur folk and the feather folk knew only too well, and so in great confusion they fled to the swamps, to the tops of the mountains, or into deep gloomy caves.

Moose was as frightened as any of the others who ran from the giants. So frightened was he that he ran up a mountain instead of into a bog. Giants can climb mountains, but they sink in bogs. Up Moose ran until he came to a great cliff, edged by a narrow trail. Here he paused to get his breath, for he was about used up.

As he stood there panting and dripping with sweat, he heard a faint peep—"Ee-eek, ee-eek"—just like that.

"Oog," snorted Moose. "Who is speaking?"

"I am," said a voice. "I, Buffalo Bird."

"Where are you?"

"Right on top of your head," answered the voice.

"What for?" asked Moose.

"To get away from the Stone Coats," answered Buffalo Bird.

"All right," answered Moose. "I'm glad to have company."

There was a crash below, and Moose knew that giants were surrounding the mountain. He looked for a place of refuge and, to his great relief, saw a narrow slit in the wall of the cliff. Into this he tried to push his head, but could not, for his antlers were far too wide.

"What will I do, Buffalo Bird?" snorted Moose, as scared as could be.

"Back in, Moose," suggested Buffalo Bird.

Moose backed in until his horns were even with the cave entrance. Here he stood with his poor frightened face looking out at the world outside. At any rate his skin was safe.

"They'll see me!" said Moose. "I don't want to be seen."

"Lie down," said Buffalo Bird. "Make your face go up and down so that it just fits in the door like a rock. Your horns will resemble an old thorn bush, long dead."

"Oh, oh," moaned Moose, tears streaming down his long, homely nose. "If they see me, they will surely kill me."

"I'll take care of that," said Buffalo Bird, but this was no comfort to Moose, for he didn't know what that meant.

After awhile there was a wild gulping sound that frightened both bird and beast out of their wits.

"What's that?" whispered Moose.

"Oggle, Oggle, Oggle-gul!" came the answer.

"Oh, it must be Turkey up in a tree," said Buffalo Bird.

"I wish he'd keep still," moaned Moose.

Down below in the valley there was a terrible racket. Stones were being crushed as giants walked over them, trees were falling with loud crashing, great boulders were being rolled into the river. The sound grew louder and louder and louder. The giants were coming up the mountain.

"Oggle, oggle, oggle-gul!" gobbled Turkey.

"Keep still," peeped out Buffalo Bird.

"They are coming, I see them," gobbled Turkey.

Scrunch, scrunch, scrunch, came the giants. Up they came by the same route Moose had taken. Moose shrank back in his cave as far as his horns would let him, and this stretched his neck terribly. Oh, if the giants should see him!

Scrunch, scrunch, they came. Rocks were crushed, and parts of the cliff fell away with the jar of their footfalls. The whole air trembled with the terror of their approach. Moose cowered flat on his stomach, his face stuck in the crack of the cave.

Soon voices like thunder were heard. The giants were talking.

"Here is a good place to stay," said one. "Let us sit down here and go to sleep."

"Here's a crack in the wall," said another voice. "It will make a good place to lean against."

On came the giants, and Moose, rolling his eyes, saw that there were two of them. On they came right to the spot where he was.

One passed the cleft in the wall, but the other sat down right against his face.

"This is a good place to camp for the night," said one with a yawn. "I'm tired after killing all those little buffaloes, elks, and bears. I think I must have eaten fifty, but still I'm hungry. A-row!" And the mountains resounded with the roar.

"What are these thorns back of me?" roared the giant. "Oh, a little thorn bush. Well, it can't hurt my coat. Nothing can pierce that."

So saying, the giant pressed back and went sound to sleep, and shortly his companion did the same.

When Buffalo Bird was satisfied that both were sound asleep, he said to Moose, "Let's kill them."

"How?" breathed Moose, his face flattened against the giant's back.

"Get Turkey to pick out their eyes," said Buffalo Bird.

"Go get him," choked Moose, half suffocated and distressed because his antlers were being pressed as flat as a piece of birch bark.

Buffalo Bird flew to the pine where Turkey was hiding and whispered to him. "Go pick out their eyes, go pick out their eyes," he said.

Turkey was too frightened even to gobble, but he agreed to try. "You peck their eyes, and Moose will rush out and trample them to death," said Buffalo Bird.

Turkey rubbed his bill on the tree, in this manner gaining great power. He poised for the dive and then flew like a kingfisher, straight for his first victim. He could not miss.

Up jumped the blind giant with a terrible roar, kicking his feet against Moose's horns and piercing the fatal spots on the soles of his feet. He fell dead.

Turkey flew at the second giant. Up he jumped with a terrible roar. He, too, kicked his feet against Moose's horns and pierced the fatal spots on his soles. Down he fell, dead.

Out came Moose, shaking his flattened face, shaking his flattened antlers, and snorting with the excitement of the sudden turn of events.

"Ho, ho!" said he. "It appears that I have killed the giants by piercing the vulnerable spots on their soles. Behold me, Moose, the conqueror of giants!"

"Not so quick to claim all the honors," said Turkey. "I am the real victor, for it was my bill that blinded the giants. I was the brave one, and but for me they would not have stepped on your spikes."

"Yes, but all the same my spikes turned the trick. But for them, the giants would still be pursuing us," retorted Moose.

"Well, they couldn't find us without eyes," snapped Turkey.

"Don't quarrel," said Buffalo Bird. "Both of you won the battle, though it was my head work."

"Yes," agreed Moose, "we both won the battle."

"But what is this 'head work' that you claim for yourself?" asked Turkey of Buffalo Bird.

"Just this," answered Buffalo Bird. "You didn't know that the red spot on a giant's foot is his only vulnerable spot. You didn't know what to do in your perplexity, but a little brown bird did, that's all."

"Fie on you," snorted Moose.

"Such nonsense," hissed Turkey.

"Come on and let's scalp the giants," suggested Moose.

So they both fell to scalping the monsters, each tearing off a shaggy scalp lock. With a bellow, Moose held up his trophy. With an oggle, oggle, oggle, Turkey held up his trophy.

"What will we do with them now?" called out Moose.

"I haven't the least idea," mumbled Turkey.

"Put them around your necks and let them hang there, brave ones," suggested Buffalo Bird.

So they strung them on thongs and hung the scalp locks around their necks. Oh, marvelous trophies of war! No one else had ever scalped Stone Coats.

Without even bidding his companions good-bye, Turkey flew down the mountain and through the trees. He gobbled to the whole world that he had fought the Stone Coats and slain them. The scalp lock fluttered against his breast, a black emblem of his valor. And today, even as then, he struts proudly and utters his foolish warwhoop, "Oggle, oggle, oggle, oggle," to impress you with his terrible reputation. And look out! He will pick out your eyes too if you get him cross.

As for Moose, his horns are still flattened and spread just as the Stone Coat pressed them when he sat against the rock. But Moose does not mind that, for he, too, wears on his neck the scalp of a Stone Coat, and it is a wonderful thing to see.

Of course, we almost forgot Buffalo Bird. Where did he go? Oh, he went where all peacemakers go. He went to a green field, far away. He is still at his head work, and may be seen among the largest of Shaggy Heads, picking away in their hair for the ticks that infest them.

So, that is how all these things came about, and the story must be true, because my grandfather of old told me so. Look for yourself, nephew, and you will see the scalp locks of Stone Coats on the necks of Moose and Turkey. Na ho!

Weasel and Old Snowy Owl

OVER THE BROWN LEAVES, AS STILL AS THE BREATH of a moth, slunk Weasel. Not a sound did he make, not a rustle of one dry leaf, for Weasel was on a raid of revenge, and old Snowy Owl should suffer.

In those days, Owl was as brown as Weasel and as skillful a hunter. So skillful was she that one stilly night she had caught Weasel's little son, Baby Weasel. This is what made Weasel furious, and now he sought his time of revenge. It came, for Weasel had discovered that Owl had two little owlets in the stub of a tree.

Weasel listened—he was always listening— whence his name, Hah-ton-das, the Listener. Up in the stub he heard the faint sounds of owlets. He listened again and heard the whir of wings in the darkness, as Owl flew from the nest hole. Owl was ready for mischief in the darkness of that moonless night, but so was Weasel.

When he was sure that the old bird was far over the pines, Weasel ran up the side of the stub and entered the hole where the fluffy owlets were. Seizing them in his cruel jaws, he snapped their necks and drank their blood. Weasel was revenged, for old Owl should grieve now.

With the same stealthy tread he slipped out of the nest and ran down the old stub, listened for a moment, and then sped to a mossy stump where, under a stone at the roots, he had his den. He wiped his lips, smiled with satisfaction, then curled up and went sound to sleep.

In the morning when he awoke, Weasel heard a plaintive moan. Old Owl could not sleep for her sorrow. Weasel was highly pleased when he heard Owl giving vent to her grief. This was music to Weasel, whose own heart had been torn. He had been well repaid for his deed!

Old Owl examined her owlets and saw that Weasel was the culprit. She now made up her mind to catch her enemy and teach him a lesson. All day long she thought about the wrong she had suffered.

Night came, and Owl flew from her nest, her keen eyes looking for Weasel. Soon she saw him curled up in a pile of leaves. Down she swooped, but just as her sharp, hooked claws were upon him, he slipped from sight and vanished like a shadow. Weasel had been listening and was waiting for just such an adventure. It was his delight to fool his pursuers.

Owl now made up her mind to start a quarrel.

"Where are you, Slim One?" she hooted. "Come out and fight."

"I am where hiding is safe," replied Weasel.

"So then you are afraid?" mocked Owl.

"Not of old round heads," said Weasel.

"Then let us run a race," said Owl. "No blood sucker can beat me."

"No night whopper can beat me," said Weasel.

"Then come out and run while I fly," said Owl.

"What is the goal?" inquired Weasel.

"Wherever you say," answered Owl.

"That hollow log over there," said Weasel.

"I'm ready," challenged Owl. "Ready—go!"

There was a whir of wings, and Owl flew for the big hollow log that lay beside a pond. Owl alighted at the hollow of one end and rushed in.

On the opposite side, Weasel rushed in at just the same moment. Then something happened. A thong closed about Owl's neck and one closed about Weasel's neck. Something had trapped them both.

The Owl strained at the cord until her eyes nearly popped out. Weasel pulled at the thong until he stretched out twice his length. But struggling was in vain.

Suddenly a long line of glowworms shed a light in the log. Both Weasel and Owl were startled to see that they were in the lodge of Jungie, one of the little folk who look just like people, but are only a span high.

A tiny curtain made of a corn husk waved aside and out came Jungie.

"I have visitors, I see," he said.

"Let me go," begged Weasel.

"Oh, oh, let me go," begged Owl.

"Not until snow flies," answered Jungie. "I am going to keep you here for awhile."

"Are you going to kill me?" asked Owl.

"Perhaps," answered Jungie. "I might need some feathers for my cap, and yours would do very well."

"Then I can go," said Weasel. "I have no feathers."

"Not so," replied Jungie. "I might need your tail for my cap. It looks very much like an eagle's feather."

"Oh, oh," moaned Owl.

"Eek, eek," squealed Weasel.

"I don't like the way you two fight," said Jungie. "I like to see all the fur folk and the feather folk keep peace."

"Oh, I love peace," said Owl.

"Oh, I love peace," said Weasel.

"Then you will smoke the pipe of peace with me?" asked Jungie.

"I will," said Owl.

"I will," said Weasel.

So Jungie brought out his peace pipe. It was of white stone and had the face of an owl and the face of a weasel carved on it. He filled it with sacred tobacco and drew fire from wood to light it.

"This is the magic house of peace," said Jungie, "and whoso enters here may have no quarrel with his foe, be he who he may. If I untie you, you cannot escape until I give you freedom. Are you ready to smoke?"

"I am," said Weasel, hoping for a quick release and a chance to dart away.

"I am," said Owl, hoping that when the thong was cut he could whirl away.

"I am not," answered Jungie, "for I have heard your thoughts. You shall stay here until the snow flies." So saying, Jungie passed through the husk curtain and the glowworms shut off their lights. All was dark.

"We will die here," said Owl. "I am choked."

"We will die here," said Weasel. "I am pulled all out of joint."

"I hope you do die," said Owl. "You ate my owlets."

"I hope you do die," said Weasel. "You killed my Weasel Boy."

"That's the way I am," answered Owl.

"That's the way I am," retorted Weasel.

"I suppose you can't help it," said Owl.

"I suppose *you* can't help it," said Weasel.

"Let us agree not to hold grudges," suggested Owl.

"That suits me," answered Weasel.

"Let's smoke the peace pipe when Jungie comes," said Weasel.

"That suits me," answered Owl.

And so, facing each other in the dark, the two agreed that each was entitled to do as he pleased, even to killing the other. It was the way of the hunter.

Snow came at last, and the hollow log lit up again. The husk curtain parted and out came Jungie.

"Are you ready to smoke?" asked he.

Both were ready and eager. The ceremony was soon over and Jungie again spoke.

"You are both bloody hunters," he began. "Both of you make war. You cannot help it, I cannot help it. It is ordered by the very way of things. You entered my house unbidden. Do you know the enchantment that lies in hollow logs?"

"I never knew," answered Weasel, squirming.

"Nor I," hooted Owl, her throat feeling a lump.

" 'Tis this," Jungie said. "Whoso passes through a magic log that's hollow, without knocking off any of the crumbly wood of the walls, gains a white coat, for nothing of color leaves the log, if not touched by the wood. You shall leave here changed into white-coated creatures."

"But then we'll be ghosts," quavered Weasel.

"I'll be a ghost of the night," moaned Owl.

Now if there is one thing above another for which Weasel is famous, it is for his caution. Weasel resolved to be cautious, for he did not want to be a ghost or to have ghosts after him. He bided his time. He might yet save himself.

"You are free," called out Jungie, breaking the snares that had held Owl and Weasel. "Pass each other in the center of the log and pass out to your freedom. Pass on your promises to become as white as the snow."

The two now stalked toward each other, each suspicious of treachery. They met at the middle. Weasel looked at Owl, and Owl at Weasel; then something happened.

Weasel jumped, and as he did, he kicked rotten wood all over Owl, dusting her whole body except for her face.

Weasel ran on, holding his own tail in his mouth, for he loved that black tip on his tail.

Out flew Owl, frightened half out of her wits, and away scampered Weasel. But when he was a dozen leaps from the log, the Jungie uttered a magic word which caused him to stop in his tracks.

Weasel stood transfixed. He could not move.

"You have played a trick upon me," shouted Jungie. "You took the tip of your tail in your mouth

so that it would remain black. You spattered Owl with crumbs from the log."

"Yes," answered Weasel. "I did not wish to become a ghost, nor did I wish a ghost chasing me."

"But you broke your promise!" said Jungie.

"That's my way," answered Weasel. "Cautious."

"Yes, it's your way," replied Jungie, "and because you did that, your tail will resemble a tiny eagle feather, white, and black tipped. You will be hunted forever, just for that, and the greater beings who shall come with arrows shall hunt you and wear your skin upon their shirts. Even I shall seek you out and wear your tail upon my cap for a plume."

"Those who hunt me must catch me first," answered Weasel.

And so Weasel went on over the snow, and so much like it did he seem that winter birds could not see him, and he feasted until he was filled.

Against a brown patch of rock Owl caught a glimpse of Weasel. Weasel moved his tail ever so slightly as he listened to the whir of old Snowy Owl's wings. Weasel was laughing as Owl pounced down upon him, for Weasel was moving the black spot on his tail, and that was all Owl saw as she swooped.

Owl clutched vainly at the soft snow, and far off, under a rock, Weasel laughed.

"My black tip will fool them forever," chuckled he.

The Ghost of
the Great White Stag

THERE IS A MIGHTY MOUNTAIN OF THE NORTHLANDS.
It rises from the placid waters of a beautiful lake,
and its summit catches the glint of the sun. On all
sides but one are other towering peaks, but none rivals
the mighty mountain, for here dwells the great white
stag whom no hunter can kill.

In the valley of the lake there is another glim-
mering lakelet and beyond a wooded slope, where the
forest folk have their council grounds. It is a far-off
retreat, but a safe one, and here all the fur folk meet
as friends.

In dim days long ago, Turtle was chief. It was he
who called the fur folk and the feather folk together.
Turtle was chief because his shell was thick and he
could draw in his head. A leader should be like that,
O nephew. A thick skin, ears that do not hear, and
a mouth that is shut in a shell are things that every
chief needs.

But Wolf was envious, and *he* would be chief. So now comes the story—jah-goh!

The call had gone forth, and from far and wide the animals came to the council. Something had happened. What could it be?

All through the woodland there was motion—the deer were coming.

All through the brushland there was a swaying—the mink and the beaver, the muskrats and the raccoons were coming.

All through the swampland there was a rustling—the beaver and the otter were coming.

All through the waterways there was a splashing—the turtles and the lizards were coming.

Above in the air were countless birds and above them, urging them on, was Sah-dah-gey-ah, the Great Blue Eagle, chief of all the feather folk. All creatures had answered the call of Turtle.

Through the tangles slunk Timber Wolf, the envious one. Very sly was he, for he had a reason for keeping out of sight. His plan was a deep one, and if he could but succeed, he would be chief.

It is known to all, O nephew, that in the beginning of things, every animal and every bird had a magic pouch in which it kept its magical charms that gave power. This pouch every creature wore on its neck. While it possessed this, it had power over other beasts and could not be injured.

Now it was the custom for the animals in coming to the council to place their magic pouches in a great bark dish which Turtle kept by the council fire. This meant that they had come for a council of peace and sat as equals.

Timber Wolf knew all this. It was his plan to steal the basket of power and run with it to a secret cave where he might hide it. This would weaken all the animals and they would have to look to him for favor. Oh, how they would beg to get even a little of that power back!

Timber Wolf licked his chops at the thought of how he would make his brother beasts obey. The cowering things—more than one would slide down his throat before he got through!

Timber Wolf grew eager. He could not wait. When night fell in the forest, he slunk about looking for sleepers so that he might steal their secret power even before the council was called.

He skulked around until he found Old Bear. Here was luck, indeed, for Old Bear was on his back, his paws over his eyes, and his pouch of secret power bulging from his neck. It took but a snap of Timber Wolf's sharp teeth to sever the thong that bound the pouch to the Bear—just a snap.

Timber Wolf gave a slight growl of satisfaction and bounded away to hide the magic in his own pouch. Bear was now in his power! The beginning was good. Yes, Timber Wolf was pleased.

Morning came, and all the animals and birds started on their journey again—all but Old Bear, who slept too long and arose weak and dazed. He did not know what had happened to him, but he knew that he felt sick.

He shook himself and tried to amble along, but he reeled from side to side. Still he made up his mind to keep on and never turn back, for Turtle had called a council, and Turtle was chief. This being so, Bear would obey!

At length the great day came, and Turtle saw around him a great host of tribesmen. Each sought its own group, its own corner, or its own side of the fire. Turtle stood upon a stump and looked over the throng.

"Are all here?" he shouted.

A great shout went up, "We're here!"

"I do not hear the voice of Bear," called out Turtle. "Who has seen Bear? Perhaps, like White Stag, some traitor has slain him."

No one answered, but all remembered the tragedy of White Stag.

"Those who fail shall be without the new power," said Turtle. "Oh, all ye who are friends, place your magic power pouches in the great basket of friendship. Sit here as equals."

One by one the beasts and birds put their pouches

into the basket. Even Timber Wolf put in a pouch—
but kept one slyly hidden. It was his own, so that he
could betray Turtle when the moment came.

Turtle surveyed the basket and spoke again. "I
see the pouch of Bear but not of Timber Wolf," said
Turtle. "Nevertheless I see Timber Wolf here and
do not see Bear. It appears that mischief has come
upon us."

You see, Turtle was very wise.

"How do you know that Bear's pouch is there
and that mine is missing?" growled Timber Wolf,
edging close to the basket.

"Because Turtle is chief, and Turtle is wise,"
came the answer.

Wolf gave a snarl and sprang at Turtle, tipping
him over and throwing him upon his back on the
ground.

All the animals leaped toward Wolf, who turned
round and round, showing his fangs. But not a fur
folk or a feather folk could touch Timber Wolf, for
all power to fight was in the basket of friendship.

"Stand back," growled Timber Wolf. "Behold
your chief sprawling on his back, overthrown by a
swish of my paw! A fine chief is he. His dignity is to
be admired! Oh, able leader of all the wood folk, how
neatly you spin upon your shiny shell! How yellow
your breastplate, how beautifully marked! How your
stubby hands and feet clutch at the air, appealing to

the clouds to turn you over. Ho ho, ho ho!"

Timber Wolf now sprang to the stump and began to address the wood folk. "Obey me," he shouted,
"and I shall lead you forth to make war!"

There was a sudden sound behind him, and
Timber Wolf gave one swift glance over his shoulders.

He saw Turtle extend his head, dig his nose in
the earth, give a twist of his neck, and turn over with
a flop.

Timber Wolf's mouth opened and his tongue
hung out, for Turtle now leaped into the air and
came down upon the basket of friendship with a
splash. As he landed, all the pouches of power popped
out like seeds from a snapdragon pod, and flew back
where they belonged. One flew far, far into the forest,
and struck the neck of poor Old Bear, limping along
so slowly.

Immediately all the animals growled and rushed
upon Timber Wolf, holding him prisoner in a circle
of extended claws and sharp teeth. Timber Wolf was
in for it, and knew his time had come.

Turtle Chief mounted the stump. "Hold the
prisoner while I give you the great news," said he. "I
have called this council to tell you that the Ongwe
are coming, the mighty *Ongwe Oweh,* who are wiser
than all the wood folk."

"Who are the Ongwe, that we should consider

their coming?" snapped Timber Wolf from the circle.

There was rustle and a snort. Into the council square leaped Old Bear.

"Oh, chief," shouted he, "I have been greatly wronged and by trickery delayed. My power was stolen, but by magic came back to me. Still, my delay has shown me a great thing. The Ongwe are coming."

"The Ongwe!" shouted all the animals. "Who are the Ongwe?"

"I was about to tell you," shouted Turtle. "The Ongwe are men-beings, and they are going to hunt, and there is one whom they shall hunt because they will hate him. He is Timber Wolf."

Timber Wolf snarled, and with a sudden spring he leaped high over the heads of the beasts around him. He dashed for the mighty mountain, swimming the lake, skulking the brushland, and then scaling the peak. Here he found refuge in a dark cave—it was a den to his liking, for he could look down upon the council and lay his schemes against it.

"What shall we do now?" asked Turtle, when the excitement had died down.

"Let us hunt Timber Wolf and revenge ourselves," cried many voices.

"Let us catch him and leave none among us for the Ongwe to hate," cried others, planning to tear him limb from limb.

And so it was that all the birds and animals scat-

tered in the forest, looking for Timber Wolf. But
when night had come, not one had seen him, though
Timber Wolf had seen them all.

Wolf now crept into his dark cave, but drew
back with a sharp cry. Before him in the darkness
were two glowing eyes of evil. Someone was spying
on him!

He turned and fled to the mountainside, where
he cowered behind a great rock. But here was a rustle,
a constant rustle. Who could be here? Spies were
everywhere!

Wolf now slunk along with greater caution to
an open space where the moonlight fell. Here he
could see his foes if any appeared. But what was that?
A great black shadow waved over the ground.

Wolf's hair rose in a shaggy crest from his neck
to his tail. The black shadow beckoned and swayed.
Then there came a creak and a groan, "Djis-gaah,
djis-gaah!" So came the sound, and it was a word
meaning *ghost!*

Timber Wolf looked up at the moon and gave a
long despairing howl. His whole body trembled.

"Oh, to escape this awful place!" So thought
Wolf, as he crept away from the open and sought
refuge behind a great pine. Here he heard a rattle
and, looking down in the dim light, saw the bones of
the great elk he had stalked in the snow and slain
only the winter before when the council had gathered.

The bones glinted a white in the dim light filtered through the branches.

Timber Wolf felt a chill gripping his very marrow, and with mincing steps he crawled out from the bone pile. Again he sought the open, but no sooner had he reached the clearing than he saw a great patch of white, like a cloud, slowly moving through the open spaces. It seemed to grow large and then small, and a portion waved up and down.

Timber Wolf grew cold with terror and stood as
if frozen to the ground. The ghostly white thing came
nearer and nearer.

Wolf could not move now and his jaws grew
hard. The ghost was upon him! There was. a crash.
He felt himself lifted high and borne away, nor could
he even struggle, for a great spear was thrust through
his lower jaw and another through his hind leg. Only
a faint whimper escaped from his throat as he felt
himself carried on and on and on.

Down in the council circle, a great fire blazed
and all about it were the faithful fur folk discussing
the coming of the Ongwe. Suddenly Turtle Chief
raised his hand.

"Someone is coming," said he. "Be still."

There was a cracking of sticks and the dashing
of swift feet. Then into the glare of the light leaped
the great White Stag, Timber Wolf pinned in his
antlers.

"I have come," began White Stag. "I have come
with the culprit who disobeyed the laws of friendship
and who sought power by theft."

"Deliver him to us," shouted all the fur folk.

"I give him to you," answered the White Stag.
"Let him forever be despised and hunted. Know
you that last year, when winter came, and we gathered in council, Timber Wolf took me as I slept and
killed me. I am the ghost of him you once called

Great White Stag. I am now the spirit of this mountain and watch over it. When the moon shines over the peak, you will see me leaping through the clouds and now and again leaping down the mountainside into the water."

"Oh, Great White Stag," said Turtle, "you have done a good deed. Your slayer shall be punished. When the Ongwe come we shall suffer, perhaps, but Timber Wolf shall suffer more, for we shall call out to the Ongwe when Wolf prowls round."

"Be gone, Timber Wolf," called out Turtle. "Know that you are hated and despised."

"I go," snarled Timber Wolf, "and I go hating all of you."

"Farewell," called out Great White Stag, leaping into the air and up to the clouds.

The fur folk and the feather folk looked in amazement as their friend sped away. As they watched, they saw him descend from the clouds and drop down upon the mountain he loved.

"He was Great White Stag," said Turtle Chief, "but henceforth we shall call him by a new name. It shall be White Face, for it is the law of the forest that once gone to the spirit world, the earth-name may not be used."

And so forever after, all the forest folk looked up to the mountain and called out to their friend White Face, who dwelt there.

When the Ongwe Oweh Indians came, they often saw White Face leaping from crag to crag, up in the air and down into the lake. Well did they know their arrows never could reach him, for White Face was a ghost.

In the days when wisdom came and Ha-yo-wen-tha brought the truth, the story of White Face came to men, and then all who were Ongwe Oweh went out to hunt timber wolves and kill them.

The wolves have gone from the great forest, and not one ever visits the mighty mountain now, but the spirit of Great White Stag may still be seen. It is he who guards the mountain, the lake, and the valley, and brings peace.

Look on a starry night when the sky is bright and the moon is low—look above the mountain, and you, too, shall see the ghost of Great White Stag. Na ho.